THE RAVEN

HARRY STARKE GENESIS BOOK 2

BLAIR HOWARD

THE RAVEN

By

Blair Howard

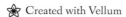 Created with Vellum

DEDICATION

This one is for my daughters Mallory, Jennifer, Kathryn and Sarah.

Sandra McDowell held her purse tightly under her arm as she crossed the dimly lit parking lot. She'd just completed a long day and then a long night of boring but necessary work for the Hamilton County School Board, of which she was a member.

They'd spent the day discussing everything from this year's budgets and grants, to special commendations and scholarships for the County's most advanced students. A lot of money talk, a lot of arguing, and a lot of animus. She was exhausted.

Sandra and her husband were quite wealthy... No, they were extremely wealthy, churchgoing, all around good people, and thus were involved in numerous charities. She and her husband were philanthropists so it had always been easy for her to give money away. She would have liked to do more: finance scholarships for education, for instance, and she could, but to do so was a bureaucratic nightmare—so many hoops to jump through that it left her exhausted—so she didn't.

She was in it for the children, because she believed that

she could be a force for good in the American education system, to help kids, including her own daughter Chelsea, learn and become the best that they could be. Unfortunately, being part of the system included talking money.

But the long day was over, and as she walked to her car, the clickety-clack of her heels on the pavement was the only sound to be heard echoing across the lonely parking lot.

It was ten after eight, the moon was up, white and round in the sky, and the cold night air made Sandra shiver. Or was it more than just the cold air? She'd always felt safe in that particular neighborhood, but that night she couldn't rid herself of the feeling that someone was watching her.

Must be the full Moon messing with my head, she thought, and a smile touched her lips. She wasn't superstitious and yet... the uneasiness persisted.

She pressed a button on the key fob, the lights on the Mercedes flashed, the locks clicked, and she quickly opened the door, climbed inside and locked the doors, surprised to find herself a little out of breath.

Don't be stupid, Sandra, she thought. *You're being paranoid!*

She looked around the deserted parking lot: nothing, just a half-dozen cars parked in their assigned spots close to the building. Mentally, she shrugged, then pushed the button to start the hybrid engine. The headlights came on but again, much to her relief, revealed nothing.

Oh come on, Sandra. You're being stupid.

She put the car into drive and it rolled silently out onto the highway. She glanced at all three rearview mirrors and was relieved to see that no one was following her.

She applied pressure to the pedal, the gas engine kicked in, and the car surged forward toward Taft Highway and home.

Sandra loved driving at night. Being safe inside her car helped her feel more at ease, relaxed. She turned up the radio; soothing jazz filled the air. She hummed along with the tune, already anticipating a glass of red wine, a hot bath, and, finally, an hour relaxing with a good book. It had been a while since she'd allowed herself such luxury, and she couldn't get home soon enough.

It was dark, the highway almost deserted. This was no time to be speeding, especially within the city limits, so she drove five miles below the speed limit, staying in the right-hand lane, glancing every now and then at all three rearview mirrors, halting at every stop sign and red light. *Better safe than getting a ticket.*

Suddenly, the jazzy melody on the radio was drowned out by an ear-splitting *VROOOM*, and the inside of the car and all three rearview mirrors were lit up by a brilliant white light, blinding her. There was no escaping it, the light, and she had to squint to see the road ahead. It was as if a semi-truck had crept up behind her and was not-so-subtly demanding she move out of the way.

"What are you *doing?*" she muttered. "Just come on past me, okay?"

But whoever was driving the floodlights made no attempt to pass. Instead, the vehicle—Sandra assumed it was one of those oversized pickup trucks—surged closer to her, uncomfortably close. Instinctively, she stepped on the gas, the big car surged up to and beyond the speed limit.

"Cut it out you... doofus!" she yelled at the mirror. The floodlights surged again, came within inches of her rear bumper, then dropped back.

Oh, dear Lord, he's playing with me.

Again, she glanced up at the mirror and... *Oh dear. Here he comes again...* Bam!

Her head slammed back against the headrest, then jerked forward, causing her to lose control of the wheel, but only for a second, and then she realized what had happened: the madman had rear-ended her!

She was scared, really scared. Her heart beating as if it would jump out of her chest. She turned on her emergency lights, put her foot on the brakes, and brought the car to a stop on the hard shoulder, her hands still clutching the steering wheel, her knuckles white. The floodlights pulled off the road behind her and came to a stop some fifty feet to her rear.

Okay, Sandra," she told herself. *Get a grip of yourself. It's just a fender bender, annoying, but nothing to worry about. Just exchange insurance info, and you'll be on your way.*

She took the papers from the glove compartment and her phone from her handbag and stepped out onto the hard shoulder.

The big vehicle's headlights seemed even brighter, so bright she couldn't look at them directly. She shielded her eyes with her left hand and, keeping the big vehicle within her peripheral vision, she made her way slowly to the rear of her car. She glanced down at the rear of her car. The right-side taillight was broken and there was a nasty dent in the trunk lid.

"Hello," she said when she saw the passenger door of the big vehicle open. "What a night, huh? You hit me."

Oh, boy, did he ever? she said to herself, trying to make light of it, but she was becoming angrier by the second, because the man now approaching, a silhouette against the truck's headlight, still had not said a word.

"Okay, listen," she said, "It's just a ding. Here's my paperwork, I'll—" Her eyes widened; instinctively, she raised her arm, and a millisecond later, something hard smashed into her head and left wrist.

She staggered backward, fell to her knees, grazing them on the cold, rough asphalt. She fell over sideways, her head spinning, her right hand on her left wrist, her eyes tight shut, teeth clenched from the pain, blood coursing down her face. She wanted to cry and couldn't...

The man stood over her, frozen, the tire iron raised above his head. Sandra let out what she thought was a scream, but her own voice sounded to her as if she was underwater.

And so did another voice, a man's voice, when he said, "Geez, can't you do anything right. Here, give that to me, you idiot!"

He grabbed the tire iron, stood over Sandra, who looked up at him through a curtain of blood, and then he struck her again.

And again.

And again.

And...

Sandra McDowell's head fell back onto the asphalt, and then... nothing.

2

I woke early that December morning in 2008, a
Tuesday, as I recall. You know those mornings, right?
When you wake up on the *right* side of the bed? You
open your eyes and just know it's going to be a great day.
Yeah, it was one of those mornings, unseasonably warm,
dry, and calm weather for early December. A cool breeze
streamed in through the open window, the sun shining, the
birds chirping.

I went to the kitchen, made myself a huge cup of coffee,
black, and a generous breakfast: scrambled eggs, sausage,
bacon, the whole shebang. After I ate, I took my coffee out
onto the balcony of my condo and was gifted by one of those
amazing scenic views of the Tennessee River. The sun was
still at a low angle and played on the water, turning it into a
magical river of golden ripples, and I couldn't have imag-
ined a nicer morning.

I'd been an ex-cop for only a few months, and only three
weeks earlier had closed my first case as a PI, so waking up
early was still wired into my brain. That morning, I didn't
complain.

My plan for the day was painfully simple. First, I'd make another cup of coffee. Then, I'd shower, dress in something comfortable and drive to the office—I run a private investigation agency, and we have an office in downtown Chattanooga, a few blocks from the Flatiron Building on Georgia Avenue. I'd listen to voicemail on the way there, make a few calls, and arrive at work ready for the new day. Brilliant. I couldn't hold back a smile.

I should've known then I was jinxing it—who wakes up with a dumb grin on their face? And at six-thirty in the AM, no less.

I'd finished my coffee and was headed back to the kitchen when my phone rang in the bedroom. I put the cup down next to the coffee machine and went to answer it.

It was my father, which immediately tipped me off that something wasn't right. You know my father, right? August Starke. Today he's a superstar attorney, but even back then in 2008 he was huge, and a call from him so early in the day likely meant he wasn't calling to wish me good morning, something he rarely, if ever, did.

"Harry?" he said, in a voice that told me he was wide awake and had been for a while.

"Morning, Dad, what's up?"

"Umm, yes, good morning... Harry, I need you to meet me at the Country Club today."

"I appreciate the invitation, Dad, but today—"

"This isn't a social call, Harry. This is serious."

I stopped what I was doing and listened.

"It's Jim McDowell. His wife, Sandra... she's dead, Harry. She's been murdered."

My skin crawled. I didn't know Sandra that well—I'd seen her a few times at social events, and once at one of my father's birthday parties—but I knew Judge McDowell was one of August's closest friends, which made it personal.

"When do you want me to be there?" I said, mentally putting all my other plans for the day on hold.

"Ten o'clock. I'll be in the restaurant."

"I'll be there."

"Thanks, Harry."

He hung up, and I put the phone down.

Damn.

I'm Harry Starke, by the way. Before becoming a private investigator I'd been a cop with the Chattanooga Police Department for more than ten years, nine of them a detective, so death was nothing new to me. I'd lost colleagues, and civilians, and three weeks earlier, during my very first case as a PI, I'd lost an informant, who was only a kid... But it was still hard to get over the thought that someone close to your family was dead. I knew Sandra McDowell was a loving wife and mother, and that she was beloved in the community. I'd never heard a bad word about the woman.

Why the hell would somebody want to kill her? I thought.

Jim McDowell was a District Court Judge, and a bona fide hard-ass, a present-day equivalent of Judge Isaac Parker —the hanging judge. Jim had made dozens, if not hundreds, of enemies throughout his career, so, naturally, my thoughts jumped to them.

Could this be a revenge killing by one of the criminals Jim put away? Or did Sandra have some skeletons in the closet of her own?

It was pointless to speculate about it, so I quit trying and hit the shower and then got dressed: a black T-shirt and jeans, shoulder holster with my M&P9, black leather jacket;

what I considered the well-dressed, modern-day Mike Hammer would wear... Yeah, yeah, I'm jesting. I dress for comfort, not for show.

By then it was just after nine o'clock. I sorted through some paperwork, made a couple of quick calls, and then headed out the door... *to what?* I wondered.

3

I did listen to my voicemail on the way to the Country Club, and I did make a few more calls, the first of which was to Jacque Hale.

"You're up early, Harry," she said. "You coming in?"

I had to smile. Jacque is my PA and one of the smartest people I know. She's a beautiful young woman; Jamaican, five-nine, slim, a wonderful personality, and a smile that will melt your heart. But don't let all of that fool you; Jacque has a Bachelor's in Criminology and a Master's in Business Administration, which is why I hired her, and which made her an essential part of the team.

"I'm afraid not," I said. "Something's come up, so I need you to cancel my appointments until... well, just cancel everything for today."

"Yes, of course. Is everything all right?"

"Not quite. I'm on my way to meet my father... It looks like we might have a new case. I'll update you as soon as I know more."

Twenty minutes later I drove through the tall wrought-iron gates of the Country Club and up the long sandy driveway to the main building and the restaurant. Then I parked my Maxima among the shiny Bentleys and Porsches. Maxima? Sure! And yes, I could have afforded something more... Hell, I could've afforded a Ferrari, but that would've been kind of stupid. People are quick to judge, and in my line of work, I need them to underestimate me.

Anyway, I found my father waiting for me in the restaurant drinking a cup of coffee. He stood up as I approached.

"Thanks for coming, Harry."

We shook hands. Like I said earlier, August Starke is a well-known attorney specializing in tort—a fancy name for a personal injury lawyer—which is how he started his professional career many years ago. Even back then in 2008, though he wasn't the billionaire he is today, he'd already become the scourge of big pharma. But, when he is not in the courtroom, you'd never guess it. At fifty-eight years old, my father liked to work out and, of course, play golf with his buddies and, most weekends, with me.

"How could I not?" I replied. "What's the situation?"

"Come on, I'll show you."

He left a ten-dollar bill under his coffee cup and led me through the restaurant to the back—the cigar smoking room, a place I'd rarely visited... I don't smoke. Anyway, it was one of those old-timey looking rooms, with huge leather armchairs, dim lighting, and dark paintings on the walls. It was where the rich and anonymous cut their deals and fed their cancers... Ugh!

District Court Judge James Mattoon McDowell was seated in one of the chairs with a glass in his hand. *Hard liquor at this time of day? He must be in one hell of a state.*

He looked up at me. His eyes were like two chips of ice.

"Harry, thank you for coming." He half stood, squeezed my hand, then sat back down again.

He wasn't a big man, five-eleven, hair graying at the temples, neatly trimmed mustache, slim build, but fifteen years on the bench had turned him into a stern jurist that rarely ever smiled... at least not in public.

I sat down opposite him, and August stood beside his friend, one hand on his shoulder.

"I am so sorry for your loss, Judge," I said.

"Thank you. And please, call me Jim." He mustered a momentary smile but held his composure.

"What can I do to help?"

"Find the son of a bitch who killed my wife!" he snapped.

I knew Judge McDowell as a stoic man, a man who radiated confidence and gravitas, which meant I'd have to navigate the conversation carefully.

"I'll do what I can, Jim. Can you tell me what happened?"

"Last night..." He swallowed hard. "Sandra didn't return home. I called, but she didn't pick up. By then it was almost ten o'clock. She should have been home by eight-thirty. I called her again, and again. Still no answer, so I called 911 then, and... and..."

His emotions got the better of him. He put a hand to his face, wiped tears from the corners of his eyes with his thumb and index finger.

"I apologize," he said.

August squeezed the man's shoulder. "It's okay, Jim."

"I want to hire you, Harry. How much is your retainer? Can you start today? Right now?"

"Of course, Jim," I said. "I'll do everything I can. Don't worry about the retainer, not right now, we can discuss it later."

"No, don't worry about the money," August said, looking at me. "I'll take care of it."

I frowned at him. He either didn't see it, or he simply took no notice.

Jim patted my father's hand. "Thank you, August, this means a lot." He looked up at me. "What else do you need, Harry?"

"That's all, for now. I'll get with Sergeant Gazzara and find out what she has. Go home, Jim. Try to get some rest, okay?"

It's gonna be fine, I wanted to add, but didn't. How could I? The man had just lost his wife. His life would never be the same.

The judge nodded weakly, and so did August.

"Do you need another one of those?" August asked, referring to the empty glass in McDowell's hand.

"No. I'll try to take Harry's advice," he said, rising unsteadily to his feet; stress has a way of doing that to you. "I'll go home."

"Good," August said, taking him by the arm.

"I'm fine, August," he said, shaking him off. "I'm fine..." and he turned and strode quickly from the room, back straight, head held high.

August and I followed at a respectful distance. I well knew how much of an effort the man was putting into his dignified exit.

Back in the restaurant, I put a hand on August's arm and said, "Will you listen for a minute, Dad?"

"What is it, Harry? Please don't tell me you won't take the case. If it's the money—"

"Of course I'm taking the case. But yes, it is the money. I get it that Jim's your friend, and I appreciate your support, but please, let the man pay his own bill. He can afford it, and I need him to take me seriously."

Yes, I know what you're thinking, and no, I didn't need the money. My mother died when I was fifteen, leaving me a considerable inheritance, so money wasn't the issue. But I was new to the whole "Private Investigator" thing, and it was my business, my career, so I needed to be taken seriously... And besides, I was thirty-six years old and couldn't allow my father to sponsor my business.

"I understand, Harry. I'll talk to him."

I could see the situation was weighing heavily on him, as well. I gave him a quick, one-armed hug.

"Thank you, Dad. And... you. You hang in there too, okay? I'm all over it."

"Go get the bastard, Harry," he said, and he patted my shoulder.

By the time I got out of there, it was almost noon. I gave the valet ten bucks and he fetched my car, not something I'd usually do, but the day was warm—hot, even—and I no longer felt particularly cheery. My brain was already working on a course of action, and it started, as it often did, with a call to Sergeant Catherine Gazzara.

Kate used to be my partner in the CPD and was my dearest friend. A friend with benefits, as the kids say these days... Okay, so we were dating. Besides being an extraordinarily lovely woman, Kate was one of the best cops I knew.

She picked up after a single ring. "Hey, Harry."

"Hey, Kate. Listen, are you up on the murder of Sandra McDowell?"

Kate paused for a second. "Yeah, I caught it; it's mine. How do you know about it?"

"Jim McDowell is a close friend of August's. Sandra is—

was his wife. I just learned of her death. McDowell hired me."

"Oh, geez, I'm so sorry, Harry."

"Don't worry about me. What can you tell me about the case?"

"Not much, at this point. The body was discovered around eight-thirty-five last night by a patrol car. She was on her way home from Signal Mountain. I'm still waiting for confirmation, but from what I know so far, someone rear-ended her, and when she pulled over, bludgeoned her to death."

"Damn."

"Yeah. A horrible way to go."

Neither of us spoke for a moment—a moment of silence for Sandra.

Then, Kate said, "Look, Doc Sheddon is performing the autopsy. I'm on my way there now. You're welcome to join me? I'll catch you up on what we have so far."

"Sounds like a plan. I'm on my way."

I made a right turn at the intersection, which would eventually take me to Amnicola and the Hamilton County Forensic Center, a couple blocks away from the PD.

I was there not ten minutes later and discovered, much to my pleasure, that I'd beaten Kate to it. No, it wasn't a competition, but we were both competitive, and I did get there first, so... I win, right?

I was greeted by Carol Owens, Doc Sheddon's Forensic Anthropologist and the only other person working at the Center.

"Well, well, Harry Starke," she said dryly.

"Hey, Carol, what's cooking?" A vailed reference to a part of her job that she wasn't particularly proud of, kept very quiet about in fact. She was responsible for skeletonizing the itinerate, unclaimed bodies—after a long period of waiting and searching for relatives, of course—and to do that she... Okay, I'm not going there... absolutely not.

She frowned, and I smiled.

"Lighten up, Carol, it can't be that bad. Is Doc in yet?"

"Are you kidding? Of course he is. It's almost noon, for Pete's sake. Come on," she said and led me to the autopsy room.

She didn't need to. I knew exactly where it was, having attended more postmortems there than I could count... and more than any human being should be expected to... *Ah, I thought I was done with these when I quit the PD.*

I suited up in throw-away Tyvek coveralls and entered the chamber of horrors. Doc was also suitably attired and already working—scrubs, rubber apron, face shield and mask, latex gloves, Bluetooth microphone—standing over Sandra McDowell's body.

The sight of the body hit me like a hammer: her head and face were horribly disfigured... It never got any easier and, as hardened to it as I thought I was, I still had to close my eyes for a minute and swallow hard to battle the nausea that threatened to overwhelm me.

Doc Sheddon was a small man, slightly overweight and completely bald, half-glasses glinting through the face shield. His round face greeted me with a completely inappropriate smile.

"Hey, Harry! You're right on time. You're just in time for the best part! I'm about to carve."

Now, I like to think I have a sense of humor—I've inherited some of my father's sarcasm and dry wit—but Doc Sheddon's morbid, gallows humor always made me a little uneasy.

"Hold up, Doc. Talk to me first, then I'll leave y'all to

it." I knew the procedure, of course, but that didn't mean I liked thinking about it.

Carol Owens stepped behind the table and stood to his left, next to Sandra's head, as Sheddon spoke.

"Okay, here's what we know for sure. Time of death... eight-thirty, maybe a few minutes earlier, yesterday evening. The cause of death... blunt force trauma. She was hit repeatedly on the head. Most of the blows landed on the frontal and parietal bones, fracturing them.

"The injuries are consistent with a long metal object, probably a tire iron... See, here, this round indentation in her forehead, and this one here is just the same? They appear to have been made by the head of the instrument, possibly a Red Hound lug wrench. They were—still are I suppose—standard equipment on most models. I have one in my old Ford Expedition. I can show it to you, if you like."

I knew exactly what he was talking about. I had one in the trunk of my Maxima, a steel bar with a screwdriver-like tip at one end and a curve at the other ending in a socket wrench for the lug nuts.

"Nah, I know what you're talking about. Carry on, Doc."

"Interestingly," he continued, "her left wrist is also shattered."

"Yes, I see that. Defensive wound. She was trying to block the blows?" I said, thoughtfully.

"One blow, anyway," Sheddon confirmed as he stepped to the left, forcing Carol to move to the left too. "She wouldn't have been able to do much more than that because... Well, look at her knees."

I looked. Wished I didn't have to. It was still hard to look at someone I'd known and think of her as just another body. Her knees were scraped. My brain quickly made the connections.

"So," I said, "she tried to block the first blow." I raised my left hand above my head. "A strike which was hard enough to fracture her wrist and, presumably, bring her to her knees."

Owens was nodding.

"Yes," Sheddon agreed. "And then they finished the job. I count seven more blows to the head, eight in all, but it was the third one that was fatal."

"Whew..." I exhaled. "How d'you know it was the third?"

"The blows are crisscrossed... see? Here, here, here... This one, it shattered the parietal bone... caved it right in, poor woman. I don't think she would have felt it though... too far gone by then."

At that moment, the doors swung open and Kate stepped inside.

"Sergeant Gazzara," Sheddon uttered, staring at her. "You're looking as lovely as ever, my dear."

I couldn't help but agree with him. She was indeed stunning. At almost six feet, Kate had a slender figure, dark blond hair tied back in a ponytail, eyes that could see right through to your soul, and the energy of the most badass cop you could wish to meet. That day she was all-business in a black turtleneck, waist-length brown leather jacket, black jeans, and a Glock 17 and gold badge on her belt.

"Hey, Kate," I said.

"Hey, Harry. Carol. What've we got, Doc?"

"If you're staying, Kate," he said, "you'll need to suit up. If not, stand by the door and I'll bring you up to speed."

And she did, and he did.

She stood by the door as he had requested, produced

her iPhone and turned on the recording app, nodded, and folded her arms, holding the phone pointed in Doc's direction.

Doc ran through his findings for her, with interjections and theories from both me and Carol. Kate listened, nodding, frowning.

"Good job, you two," she said when Doc finally quit talking. "You too, Harry. There's still a little bit of cop left in that PI head of yours."

She winked at me, letting me know that playful Kate was still lurking about inside there somewhere. There was something about that look, that wink, that set loose a flutter of butterflies in my stomach.

"Why, thank you," I said. "What about you? D'you have anything to add?"

"I've got something, but you're not going to like it."

She tapped on her phone, and then showed me the screen. I took it from her and zoomed in on the image.

"From the crime scene?" I asked, knowing the answer before she said it.

"It is."

On the screen was a photo of a section of gray asphalt pavement with a crude "V" drawn in what could only have been Sandra McDowell's blood.

"Geez," I muttered. "Is this what I think it is?"

Kate nodded. "Sure looks like it to me. Voron's calling card."

4

"Voron... Geez... No way," I said, shaking my head in disbelief.

Vladislav Andreevich Voronov, better known by his nickname Voron, which means "raven" in Russian, was an assassin, a hitman, a killer for hire. His clients? The Russian mafia. During his tenure with that organization, he was one ruthless SOB, carried out more than three dozen proven executions and was suspected of at least that many more. The letter "V" was his calling card. Left next to his victims' bodies, it was often drawn in their blood and meant to be a stark warning to the rival mobs, crooked cops, politicians, what have you. The mark I was looking at now looked scarily similar.

There was only one problem, though: Voron had been on death row since the late eighties. In fact, his execution was imminent, and all over the news.

I looked at Kate.

"Yes," she said, reading my mind. "I know what you're thinking. How could it be Voron when he's in jail awaiting his visit from the grim reaper?"

row? I think I can make it before they close up shop tonight."

"Tell me you're not jumping on the next plane to talk to a serial killer."

I beamed. "You're kidding? This is the most excitement I've had in two weeks. You want to come along?"

"As tempting as that sounds, Harry," she said sarcastically, "some of us have real police work to do."

"This is real police work, Kate," I said, a little hurt by her dig at me. "I'm a licensed private investigator. Jim McDowell hired me. So I'm officially on the case. Either way, someone has to talk to Voron, and I trust you got things covered on this end."

"You know I do." She smiled, and I was again assaulted by a flutter of butterflies.

Geez, how I wished... Well, I couldn't, she couldn't, wouldn't, and I had a plane to catch, if I could get a seat.

"I'll be back tonight," I promised.

"I'll call Nashville and let them know you're coming," she said.

"Thanks, Kate. I owe you."

"And don't you forget it... I'll be round tonight to collect."

She got into her car, and I got into mine. The day had just gotten a whole lot more exciting.

Sometimes, it's the little things in life that make you happy. I couldn't help but smile the whole fifteen minutes it took me to get to the airport.

What the hell are you smiling about? I thought as I turned into the short-term parking lot. *The man's a frickin' killer... and this ain't Silence of the Lambs, you jerk.*

I've seen my share of killers back when I was with the CPD, but few of them... strike that, none of them were of

Voron's caliber—no pun intended. He was the ultimate assassin—a professional killer for hire, the kind of guy Vito Corleone would pay the big bucks to take care of a problem. And, boy, would Voron ever take care of it.

Chattanooga is a small town, with a small-town airport, but it was better than most. I was able to grab a burger and a tall glass of beer before my flight, and when I boarded the small commuter plane, I fell asleep almost right away.

Forty-five minutes later, I landed at Nashville International Airport. I had no bags with me so it was easy on, easy off. I stopped at Starbucks in the airport mall to grab a cup of strong coffee to wake myself up. It was just after two PM and I was full of nervous energy again.

5

K ate had texted me to let me know that an Officer Malone had been assigned to meet me outside the baggage claim area, and the officer was, indeed, waiting there for me. She was leaning against a white Ford SUV with "Davidson County Sheriff" emblazoned in gold across the doors.

"Sergeant Starke," she said, holding out her hand. "I'm Officer Ruth Malone. Nice to meet you."

"Likewise, Officer," I said as I shook her hand, then slid into the passenger seat.

Malone was a small woman, maybe twenty-two years old, if that, with white-blond hair—obviously right out of a bottle—blue eyes, and pink lips. Her tentative smile and the way she held the steering wheel at ten and two, told me I was probably one of her first assignments, if not *the* first assignment.

"You can call me Harry, Officer. And I'm not with the PD anymore. I'm in the private sector." I grinned.

I won't lie, I really liked the sound of that. It sounded serious, prestigious even, the kind of phrase any government employee heard and immediately thought of as important, with a large salary and a nice car. Yeah, right!

Riverbend Maximum Security Institution in Nashville is a dour, intimidating complex of lookalike, tan-colored buildings, a prime example of unimaginative, municipal architecture. Malone dropped me off at the curb in front of the main entrance.

"Thank you, Officer," I said leaning inside the passenger side door after I stepped out of the cruiser. "Drive safe, okay?" Then I smiled at her, to put her at ease. She was a good kid.

I entered the reception area and was met by two armed guards.

"Hey, guys," I said. "I'm Harry Starke. I'm expected, I hope."

Both men nodded, and one escorted me to the clerk's window where I signed my name in the visitors' log and received my visitor's badge. One of the guards checked the log, my new badge, nodded, turned his back to me, and made a call I couldn't hear. They were obviously expecting me because just a few seconds later, a third armed guard entered and told me he would escort me to death row.

Thank you, Kate!

"What's with the extra security?" I asked as we walked.

"The inmates are all wound up," he replied. "The scuttlebutt is that as soon as your guy kicks it, they're going to riot. He's somehow gotten into their heads, if you ask me." The guard shrugged. "Which no one ever does... That frickin' Russkie will be the end of us, I reckon."

"A riot?" I asked.

"Some bullshit like that. They've been warned, but what are you gonna do, right? The jail will have to go on lock-down, probably."

"Thanks," I said, as the steel door squealed when he opened it.

"Welcome to death row," he said pleasantly, with a smirk.

It sounds brutal, like a slaughterhouse or something, but in reality, it wasn't that much different from a regular jail block, just one story, a cold walkway with cement floors, a brick wall with narrow windows on our left, and narrow cells on our right. I'd expected to be greeted by animals, like that scene in *Silence of the Lambs*: dirty, half-naked men, who would scream obscenities, maybe even spit at me, but that was not the way it was at all.

I glanced sideways into some of the cells and saw men of different ages, most of them asleep on their narrow cots, some reading. One guy was painting. None of them paid me any attention, which was a huge relief.

Finally, the guard stopped in front of the second to last cell on the block.

"Voronov, you got a visitor," he yelled with visible distaste for the inmate.

Voron had murdered at least two cops, and part of me was surprised he'd made it this long on the inside. *Friends in high places?* That was a thought for another day.

The man was sitting behind a tiny desk writing something on a piece of paper with what looked like colored pencils. I could already see a headline: *Killer On Death Row Spends Last Days Coloring.* I held back a grin.

"I'll take it from here, thanks," I said.

The guard nodded, turned, and walked away.

"Mr. Voronov?"

He put down his pencils and stood up.

"Mister?" Voron said with a thick Eastern European accent. "That's nice to hear."

I stood out of reach, maybe three feet from the bars. The cell was dim, but even in those conditions I could see that Voron was well past his prime. In his late sixties, he was smaller than me, maybe five-eleven, and a lot thinner. His head was bald, except for a few hairs over his ears and at the back of his neck, as silver as his pointed beard. He wore reading glasses and squinted when he stepped up to the bars.

"How may I help?" he said in a soft voice.

He stood proudly, back straight, head held high. I had to remind myself he was a stone-cold killer.

"Please," he said. "Come closer, I'm hard of hearing."

Like hell, you are.

I took a step forward.

"Do you know why I'm here, Mr. Voronov?"

"Not the slightest idea, Mister..."

"Starke, Harry Starke. I'm a private investigator."

The killer shrugged.

"Private investigator, huh? On what case, Mr. Starke?"

"Someone murdered Sandra McDowell," I said, watching for the tell.

His face was a stone, but I caught his eyes narrow slightly, questioningly.

He doesn't know what the hell I'm talking about? Or does he... Is he surprised that I'm onto him already? There was no way I could know.

"When did that happen?" he asked.

"Last night. Are you telling me you haven't heard?" I said, trying to read his face and failing. *No? Really? What the hell else do you expect from a professional killer?*

"How could I? It wasn't on the news this morning, and nobody is too eager to share such things with me. What happened?"

He seemed genuinely interested. *Or does the old bastard simply want to enjoy the gory details of his revenge?*

"Somebody beat her to death with a tire iron, Mr. Voronov."

"*Bozhe moi,*" he muttered, and his hand drew a small cross in the air.

"Whoever killed her signed his handiwork with a letter "V" drawn in her blood next to her body. Does that ring a bell? Any comment?" I watched his eyes.

"I know nothing of this, Mr. Starke." He opened his hands, palms up. "I've been inside these four walls for a very long time."

"Are you saying the Raven doesn't have friends on the outside? Must be lonely," I said, grinding my teeth. Either he was telling the truth, or incarceration had made him a world-class actor. I opted for the latter.

"I have friends on the outside, of course; that's not a secret. But they are not what you think. Voron, the Raven, is no more. We are all retired, Mr. Starke. I read books. I write—"

"Drop it, Voron," I interrupted him. "Don't give me the 'I've found God routine.' That BS, it won't fly with me." I took another step closer to the bars and, in a low voice, said, "Who did you hire to do your dirty work? You got what you wanted. The man's devastated, destroyed. How does it feel, Voron, revenge? How does it feel to know that the man who put you away is in agony?"

I half-expected him to crack, to smile at me, but he merely frowned, slowly shaking head, eyes cast down, his nose twitching slightly.

What's with this guy? He's like a frickin' stone; no reactions... no emotions. Is he angry? Pissed off? Is he considering making a grab for me? Or is it that he just doesn't give a damn?

He stared at me stoically for a moment then shook his head again and said gently, "I have no interest in revenge, Mr. Starke. I am sad for Judge McDowell. He was just doing his job. I hold no grudge against him, nor do I hold a grudge against his poor wife, God rest her soul. Now, my time is short and I want to be alone. It's time for you to go, Mr. Starke. I understand you have an investigation to run, but I cannot help you. So go, then. Go, my angry friend, and good luck to you." And with that, he returned to his desk and sat down.

"Don't turn away from me, you sick bastard!" I said, loud enough for the rest of the cell block to hear me. "How did you do it? Come on, you can tell me. What've you got to lose?"

He looked up at me. I could see the steely eyes glinting in the half-light of the cell.

"Leave me alone, Mr. Starke. I've nothing more to say to you."

It was then that the guard returned and put a hand on my shoulder, startling me.

"Time's up, Mr. Starke."

I shook his hand off.

"We're not done, Voron," I said, frustrated, and I left him there staring after me.

Was the trip worth it? Not hardly. I'd had the last word, but had I learned a damn thing? No. One thing was for sure, though: if Voron had any feelings at all about Sandra McDowell's death, he'd kept them well hidden. Had he put out the hit? I didn't know, and after his little speech, I was beginning to wonder, but not for long. The man was all subterfuge. It was his stock-in-trade.

On my way back to the airport—I took a cab this time—I dialed Tim Clarke, my tech guy... Okay, so he's a hacker. Well he was, and brilliant. The kid—he's seventeen—was born speaking binary. Half the time I can't understand what the hell he's talking about, but he's the best at what he does, which is why I hired him.

Tim's an expert at finding people, and by "finding" I mean "locating." And there were some people I needed to locate, but first, I had to find out who the hell they were.

He picked up after the first ring. "Hey, Mr. Starke."

"Tim, I told you, you can call me Harry. Listen, I have a job for you."

"Of course, um, Harry. What do you need?"

I heard the staccato clickety-clacking of his keyboard and had to smile. *What the hell is he doing? I haven't said anything yet.*

"Tim, you there?"

"I am, Harry. Oh, wow, you're in Nashville? That explains why you're not at the office."

I swear, if machines ever rise, Tim Clarke will be their king!

"I'm not even going to ask," I said. "Okay, listen up. I need you to find out everything you can on Vladislav Voronov, aka Voron. His past and present associates, where they are, their movements, everything. You know the drill."

He was typing as I spoke.

"And, Tim?"

"Yes, Harry?"

"Voron is a nasty piece of work, so, you stay out of places where you—and the rest of us—could get into trouble, okay?"

"In and out like a ninja, Harry. Download almost complete."

I let out a short laugh. "Do I even wanna know what you've hacked this time?"

"Nothing I haven't hacked before."

I could picture Tim at his battle station: a tall, skinny kid in front of a half-dozen monitors and a laptop, tapping and clicking, and probably watching some show on one of them.

"Thanks, Tim. I'll take a look at the files when I get back into town. Okay, I have another call coming in; we'll talk later."

I hung up on Tim and glanced at the screen. It was Rose.

Rose is August's wife, my "stepmother." Some people like to call her his "trophy wife," but although she's twenty years younger than August, and just three years older than me, she's nothing of the sort. She's a good woman, and she loves my father deeply and sincerely, and I love her for it. That being said, I wasn't someone she called that often.

I answered the call.

"Hey, Rose. Is everything all right?"

"Yes, but I need to talk to you, Harry. It's important."

My heart skipped a beat.

"What is it, Rose? Is it Dad? What's happened?"

Being away from home suddenly felt like being on another planet.

"August is fine, Harry, don't worry. But I do need to talk to you. It's about... Sandra."

I could hear her voice shake.

"Yes, I know. It's terrible," I said. It wasn't my best effort, I agree but... "What is it you want to tell me?"

"Not over the phone, Harry. I'm at home. Can you..." She sniffed a couple more times, but left the question hanging.

"Hmm, sure, but I'm out of town. Can it wait until tomorrow morning?"

"Yes, that sounds perfect, but not here. I'll meet you for coffee at Benedict's, around eleven? I have a few things I need to do first."

I'd planned on being at the office, but... "You got it, Rose. I'll see you at eleven."

"Thanks, Harry. Bye."

The phone blinked off. I stared at it, unaware of the countryside flashing by outside the cab windows, lost in thought.

Whatever it was she wanted to share with me must be pretty important. Why couldn't she talk about it over the phone? And why not at home? She doesn't want August to hear it, I thought. *Hmmm.*

I didn't like the sound of that at all. The idea of going behind my father's back made me feel decidedly uncomfortable. *Geez, what's she up to, I wonder?*

But that was for tomorrow.

6

The return flight gave me time to think about the case. I still didn't have much to go on, but one thing made sense: I was, once again, convinced that Voron had to be somehow connected to Sandra's murder. Revenge for his upcoming execution was as good a motive as any. As for opportunity, well, he wouldn't be the first inmate to orchestrate a hit from behind bars. All I needed was to find the missing links, to tie it all together. It sounded almost too easy, but hey, not all murder cases have to be tricky, right?

Right! But this one was, as I was soon to find out.

I picked up my Maxima from the short-term lot and drove straight home. I was tired and starving. It had been a long day, and the flying and the time change both ways— even if it was only an hour—made the trip feel like three separate long days.

My phone buzzed in my pocket. It was the one person I was happy to hear from.

"Hey, Kate," I said. "I just walked in the door."

"How did it go?" she asked. "You know what, don't tell

me. I'm on my way. You can tell me all about it when I get there."

"Wow, okay. That's the best news I've heard all day."

"See you." She clicked off.

The day could yet be salvaged! I'd been planning on taking a shower and going to bed early, but... Oh come on; what would you do?

I met her at the front door, and it was easy to see that she was off duty: gone were the turtleneck and jeans, exchanged for a simple white dress cut a couple of inches above her knees, and a short black leather jacket. She looked incredible.

"What's the occasion?" I said, unlocking the door.

"Just back from a date," she said.

"Oh, are you, now?" I said, smiling.

"Or maybe I'm getting ready for one." She leaned in close, kissed me, and then waltzed right on in.

I grinned to myself and followed her.

She made a face. "You better go get ready, too, Harry," she said. "You stink like a junkyard dog."

"Shower it is. Grab yourself a beer, or a glass of red. There's an open bottle on the kitchen counter. I'll be right back."

Twenty minutes or so later, I found her on the couch in front of the picture windows in the living room, her knees drawn up, her arms wrapped around them, staring out at the river. Her jacket and shoes were on a chair. The white dress accentuated every curve.

"Hey," she said, letting go of her knees and swinging her legs down onto the floor. "Drink?" She picked up a glass from the side table and handed it to me—three fingers of Laphroaig, no ice.

"Hey, yourself, and thank you," I said, taking the glass and sitting down beside her.

I took a good-sized sip, swallowed and closed my eyes, savoring the fiery liquid as it hit the back of my throat.

"So," she said, "how did it go up in Nashville? Did Voron crack?"

"Oh yeah..." I sipped my whiskey. "He cracked all right. Full confession, blow by blow... No, damn it; of course he didn't crack, not even a fricking smile."

She smiled and nodded and said, "Seriously, Harry, how'd it go, really?"

"About what you'd expect. He claimed to know nothing about it, that I was the one to break it to him. He seemed... surprised, Kate." I shrugged.

"And you believed him?" she asked.

"Hell, no! You know how guys like him are—manipulative, vicious. I bet the old bastard enjoyed my visit, though he didn't show it."

She nodded thoughtfully, then said, "Well he's not going anywhere."

"Yeah, he is," I said. "Next week. He's going straight to hell."

"Oh, that's dark, Harry, even for you. But you're right, I guess... Okay, so do you want to hear what I learned about Sandra McDowell?"

I set my empty glass down on the side table and slid closer to her. "Sure, tell me."

She tilted her head, looked sideways at me, and said, "Sandra was on the School Board..."

"Uh-huh, I know that," I said, kissing her neck.

She wriggled away. "She was at the Belle Edmondson College for Women last night, with the principal and some of the teachers. Hey, stop it!"

My hands were on the back of her dress, feeling for the zipper.

"You know," I said, "how about you tell me in the morning?"

I found that zipper.

"Oh, well," she said as the back of the dress peeled open, "if you insist."

I did.

7

K ate was already up and dressed when I rolled over in bed the following morning, blinded by the sun streaming in through the curtains. There were already signs that it was going to be a beautiful day, and I could smell coffee in the cool air.

"Rise and shine, Harry," Kate called from the kitchen. "We've got work to do!"

I joined her in the kitchen, where she wasn't making breakfast. *Damn it!*

"What time is it?" I asked.

"Seven," she said. "Make yourself some toast. I need to run home and get changed. Can't show up at the office looking like this."

I looked her all over. "Please, do! I'd love to see their faces!"

"Yeah, right," she said sarcastically. "Finkle would have a conniption. Hmm, then again, maybe I should give him a thrill, watch him drool."

"Wow, listen to you," I said. "Kinda full of yourself ain'tcha?"

She grinned at me and said, "Now think about what you just said."

I did, and I had to grin too, a self-satisfied grin.

"Yes," I said. "Maybe you had better go and change. Before you do, though, you were going to tell me what you found out about Sandra."

"Only that she was at a school board meeting at Belle Edmondson until almost eight, so that fits nicely with Doc's estimate of the TOD. She must have been attacked soon after she left. So eight-thirty is about right." She shook her head. "You can imagine how it is up at the school," she said. "Everything's neat and tight. Everyone loved Sandra. Nobody saw anyone following her after the School Board meeting there."

The Belle Edmondson College for Women is one of the most prestigious schools for girls in the state, and definitely the top school in the city. I really wouldn't have expected her to find anything there.

"So," I said, "the school is a bust?"

"Looks like it... Oh, and Sandra's daughter, Chelsea, she's a student there; she'll graduate next year."

"Huh," I said. "That could be something. Does the girl have any enemies? I've seen *Mean Girls*. I know how teenage girls can get."

"First poetry, now chick-flicks? What did you do with Harry Starke? But, yeah, you don't need to tell *me* how mean teenage girls can be. Not Chelsea though. She has friends, the teachers love her, no conflicts whatsoever, so I was told anyway. The McDowell's are wealthy, but then, so is everyone else at that school."

"Right," I said and gulped my coffee.

"Any ideas?" she asked.

"Yeah, I may have a lead." I smiled.

"Spill it, Starke."

"Nothing solid yet." I shrugged. "Rose has something to tell me: something she wouldn't tell me over the phone. She couldn't talk about it at home either, so I'm meeting her at Benedict's at eleven."

Kate raised a brow. "That's... secretive."

"Oh yeah. That was my reaction, too," I said. "I guess she didn't want to talk about it, whatever it is, in front of August, and that's not like her... not at all. One more thing: I have Tim researching Voron and his cronies. I'll let you know if I hear anything promising. You have my word."

Kate tapped on her iPhone. "Okay, let me know what you find out, and I'll try talking to Jim McDowell again, see if he can give us some more names."

"Good luck," I said and headed for my room to get dressed.

I WOULD HAVE EXPECTED Rose to pick some upscale restaurant, but instead she went for Benedict's, a small cafe on the Tennessee River that only served breakfast and lunch. It had a nice view of the Market Street and Walnut Street bridges and Coolidge Park on the opposite side of the river.

I walked through the cafe and out onto the covered deck, and I had to hide a smile when I saw Rose. She was sitting at the farthermost table close to the rail. I think I already mentioned that Rose is a beautiful woman, but all that beauty was currently hidden under a long coat and a bright silk scarf that she'd tied on her head. Her eyes—and half of her face—were covered by huge sunglasses. I had a sudden feeling I was meeting with Audrey Hepburn in one of her movies. Those sunglasses made Rose look like a giant dragonfly.

"Harry!" she called when she saw me.

I did a small wave and sat down opposite her. She raised the sunglasses.

"Thank you for meeting me, Harry."

I said, "My pleasure... But really, Rose? Those are not necessary."

"Of course they are! You never know who might be watching. I mean... people from the Country Club... well. I'm not crazy! I'm having a cappuccino, Harry. What would you like?" She waved a hand to attract a waiter's attention. She didn't need to. She stood out like a... Well, you get the idea.

I ordered a breakfast sandwich and coffee.

"All right, Rose, you wanted to talk to me, so let's hear it. If it's about Sandra McDowell, it could be important."

She looked down, slightly embarrassed. She took off the glasses and the scarf, then brushed her hair back. To a passerby, not knowing that Rose was my stepmother, we must've looked like a couple.

"Well, Harry, your father and I, we pretty much know everyone at the Club, right?"

"Sure." It was true. If the Club held a prom night, August and Rose would surely be King and Queen.

"Well, we girls like to talk, and, well, gossip... you know."

Oh boy, I thought, *here we go.*

"What have you heard, Rose?" I asked. "I'm not here to judge, and you know I don't care much for gossip. No offense. All I want is to find Sandra's killer."

I could see she was near to tears.

"It's so horrible, Harry..." She took a deep breath. "I think

Jim might have been cheating on Sandra and that he still is... if it's possible to cheat on a dead person."

Now that *was* new information. Jim McDowell never struck me as a man who would cheat on his wife. He was a conservative man, a man who prided himself on his principals. I found it hard to believe he would have a mistress, or even indulge in the odd one-nighter, but hey, stranger things have happened.

"I think you'd better tell me about it," I said, as I bit into my sandwich. "Sorry, Rose," I mumbled. "You'll have to excuse me. I haven't eaten since breakfast yesterday. I'm starving."

She smiled, nodded, and said, "That's not good, Harry, you need to look after..." She caught the look I was giving her and changed course, "Some of the girls are talking about a young woman who's been visiting the McDowell residence lately, almost every day. Very attractive, tall, blond, and she doesn't look like the help. So..." She made a motion with her eyebrows that said *make your own conclusions.*

And I did. Rose and her friends have an eye for these things, and I trusted Rose's instincts.

"Well... It could be... Okay, so how long has it been going on?"

"I'm not really sure, several months though. I do know that."

"So... this woman has been visiting the McDowell home. Sandra must have known about it, her, don't you think?"

"She could have, I suppose, but not according to Emily Watson and Jessica Strange—"

"Henry Strange's wife? Oh well, if she said it, then it must be true," I said sarcastically, interrupting her.

"Harry, I know Jess can be... Oh stop it, but she does know everybody. And, well... she knows... things."

"Rose, do *you* think Jim is, was, having an affair?" My coffee had arrived, and I took a huge gulp. "I mean, from what I know of the man, it doesn't seem likely."

"I don't know anything anymore," she said. "Maybe. These last couple of days have been so tough on him. And on your father."

I nodded. "How is August, by the way?"

"He's fine. You know your father, he's handling it. He always does."

"Good," I said, already planning my next steps. "Rose?"

"What?"

"Could you keep this between us... for maybe a day?"

She frowned. "You know I can't promise that, Harry. If Kate or any of the other officers should ask, I'll have to tell them everything I told you. But if they don't ask..."

"That's fair." I smiled. "Thank you for sharing, Rose. It could be important, even if it did come from Jessica Strange. I'll look into it."

"And from Emily and Judy Olsen, too."

Now that was a surprise. I knew Judy and her husband, and she wasn't a gossip. If she'd confided in Rose, there had to be something to it.

"Humm... That's different. Okay. I really do have to go. We'll talk later. Tell August hello for me. Wait, better not, I suppose. Drive safe, okay?"

She nodded, said goodbye, and I left a couple of twenty-dollar bills under my coffee cup and excused myself.

I now had a lead, a pretty flimsy lead, I admit, but it was something, and I didn't have to remind myself that in more than fifty percent of murder cases in the US the victim died at the hands of his or her significant other. The McDowells might be upstanding citizens on the surface, but everyone has a skeleton, or two, in the closet, and maybe this one finally slipped out into the open... Quite suddenly, Voron had slid down to number two on my list of persons of interest.

My thoughts were interrupted by my phone buzzing.

"'Tim," I answered. "What do you have for me?"

Hearing the kid's voice reminded me that I hadn't been to work in two days, and it was probably time to show up.

"I've taken a close look at Voron and his associates, Harry. I got his whole life in front of me. There's some cool black-and-white photos from the late sixties here—"

"Get to the point, Tim," I barked as I approached my car.

On the other end of the line, I heard some noises as the phone changed hands. A moment later, I heard Ronnie Hall's voice.

"You need to take it easy on the kid, Harry. It's not his fault if you've been up all night."

Oh hell, he's right.

"You're right. Let me talk to him, Ronnie."

"Can't. I sent him to get coffee while I chewed your ass."

"Okay, consider it chewed. Now what?"

"There's some bad news and some good news, man."

Ronnie is a friend of more than fifteen years, the first guy I hired when I started the investigating business—was it only two months ago? Geez.

Ronnie has a background in banking—and a Master's in Economics, which made him my first choice to organize the company. He also handles our white-collar investigations, but one of his more important qualities is that Ronnie *knows people.*

"How bad is the bad news?" I asked as I drove away from the cafe.

"Not too bad, but the good news is really great."

"Let's hear it."

"The kid really did dig up everything there is to know about this Voron guy. Nasty! You sure this is where we want to be?"

"Ronnie."

"A'ight, A'ight. Look. A bunch of Voron's old associates are in Tennessee, presumably for his execution."

"Yes, so?"

"Not just in Tennessee, Harry. The bastards are right here in Chattanooga!"

"Wait, what?" I said. "That makes no sense. Voron is in Nashville."

Something clicked on the other end of the line, and the echoey quality of the sound told me I was on speaker.

"That's not all, Harry," Tim said enthusiastically, seemingly none the worse for my barking at him. "I've tracked their phones. None of them were anywhere near the crime scene at the time of the murder."

Ronnie said, "But guess where they did show up, Harry?"

"Surprise me, Ronnie."

"The Sorbonne."

"Huh?" I had to give it to him; that was indeed a surprise.

8

"The Sorbonne?" I asked.

"That's right," Ronnie confirmed.

From the name, you might think the Sorbonne is one of those fancy restaurants where I might have expected Rose to meet me. We-ll, let me tell you, you couldn't have gotten it more wrong. You would, in fact, be hard-pressed to find a sleazier bar in the entire city of Chattanooga. Yes, it's a bar—though its owner fondly calls it a club—a dive, a place of ill-repute, a claustrophobic room with black walls and a nightmarish cacophony of noises that the bar's owner, one Benny Hinkle, has the audacity to call music. Add watered-down drinks, black lighting, and... well, you get the idea.

It's a nether world where lowlifes, junkies, hookers, and small-time criminals congregate... and also college students out for a good time. Even the elite of the city have been known to patronize the place, and now it seems a cadre of ex-killers-for-hire has made it their watering hole. If all of that doesn't tip you off, then I don't know what else to tell you.

Funny enough, though, I always felt comfortable there, still do. What can I say? Keeping an eye on the dark underbelly of the city was a part of my job, and for that there was no place better to be than the Sorbonne. It was a place where I could always "find answers." If Benny doesn't know, he can find out, and quickly... for a price, of course. And yeah, over the years, I hate to admit it, but I've grown kinda fond of the fat little bastard. Back in the day though...

So, I really wasn't that surprised to learn that Voron's friends would use the Sorbonne as their hangout. Now I knew where to find them. All I needed next was a plan.

"Listen, guys," I said. "I'll be at the office in five, if you could put together a briefing—"

"Already done, boss," Tim said eagerly.

"First of all, don't call me that. Second of all, thank you."

I hung up, checked my watch. I had some time. The Sorbonne didn't open until four, which meant I had at least three hours and a lot of work to do.

I couldn't stop thinking about what Rose had told me about Jim McDowell and his possible mistress. How was I going to get to the bottom of that? I doubted Jim would tell me much, even if he admitted to having an affair, so there had to be another way.

I trusted Rose and figured she'd told me everything she and the "girls" knew, so questioning all of the other Stepford Wives at the Club would be pointless. It seemed that once again, my best bet would be to employ Tim's skills.

But that would have to wait.

"Jacque, I need coffee in the worst way; would you mind, please?" I asked when I walked into the office. The place still had the wonderful smell of a new space—new furniture, leather, and wood...

"Sure thing, Harry," she replied. "Italian Dark, black, I suppose?"

I grinned at her and nodded.

Tim was at his desk, playing some sort of live-action video game on one of his monitors, while the others displayed lines of what looked to me like an alien language that I guessed was code. Or hoped so?

"Tim, Ronnie, my office."

Tim looked up at me, smiled, poked at the bridge of his glasses with a forefinger, shoving them higher. He didn't need to do that; it was a habit. I frowned at the kid, then winked at him and hoped he knew I was playing with him.

I loved my offices. Honestly, if it weren't for the majestic view from my condo, I think I could live there.

I entered the conference room and sat down at the head of the wide, hand-crafted table, leaned back in my chair, and sipped my coffee: life was good.

Tim entered a couple of minutes later followed by Ronnie and Jacque. Tim was, as usual, loaded to the armpits: tablet under his right arm, a wire running from his phone in his pants pocket to an earbud, open laptop in the crook of his left arm, and an overfull cup of coffee in his right hand. If any one of the devices, or the cup, slipped it would take all of us to clear up the mess, but it didn't. He set his coffee gently on the table, then the laptop and tablet, stood upright, grinned around at each of us in turn, poked his glasses, then set about connecting his laptop to one of the two 60-inch flat-screen monitors on the wall.

Ronnie? He was in full IBM business mode: white shirt, blue tie, navy blazer and... a cup of tea complete with saucer, for Pete's sake.

Jacque's outfit was simple: jeans and a white blouse that

accentuated her gorgeous coffee and cream skin. She also carried an iPad, and when she sat down next to me on my right, she looked at me—I nodded—and she tapped the record app. The meeting was officially underway.

Tim sat down next to me on my left, tapped the laptop's keyboard a couple of times, and Voron's image appeared on the big screen. It was a picture of him from back in the eighties when he was twenty years younger: nicely trimmed hair, large golden frames on his nose. There would have been a certain charm to the man, had it not been for his cold, soulless eyes. Below the image, it read: *Vladislav Andreevich Voronov AKA The Raven*.

"So that's him, huh?" Ronnie said.

Tim glanced at the image. "Yeah. Looks a lot like Stan Lee, could even be his cousin or something."

Ronnie and I stared at him.

"Comic book writer?" Tim tried. "Spiderman? The Hulk? Ah, never mind."

"Tell me about Voron," I said and sipped my coffee.

"Born in Kemerovo, USSR, in nineteen-forty," Tim read from his laptop.

"We don't need his whole biography, Tim. The recent stuff, please. The eighties through present day."

Tim looked at me, uncertainly, then at Ronnie.

Ronnie scowled at me from the end of the table; I got it.

I winked at Tim, he grinned back at me, did his thing with his glasses, looked down and scrolled, then said, "In nineteen-eighty-seven, Voronov was found guilty on thirty counts of first-degree murder and conspiracy to commit murder and was sentenced to death. "Voron had a daughter, Kristina, born in eighty-two. But she died in foster care shortly after Voron was sent to prison." Tim shook his head.

"Damn," Ronnie said.

"What a waste," I said.

That girl never even got a chance at a normal life—at any life—and all because her dirtbag of a father chose the life of a killer. At moments like that, I couldn't thank August enough for the life I'd had as a child.

"So. Voron?" I asked. "Who's he been talking to in the last twenty years? Lovers? Colleagues?"

Tim nodded. "A ton of people over the years, but mostly these three, especially in the last couple of weeks."

Tim clicked, and three more photographs appeared on the screen: all men in their sixties, Eastern European-looking, and not at all friendly.

"I present to you Tesak, Brick, and Paper Boy. All three were part of Voron's inner circle, all contract killers for the Russian and Italian mobs, but they are now retired."

"There's no such thing as a retired hitman for the mafia," I said.

Killing people for a living wasn't the kind of job where you could hand in a couple of weeks' notice, and the better you were at it, the harder it was to get out. I'd heard the three names before, in connection with Voron, and if the circumstantial evidence against them was to be believed, they were the cream of the crop.

Tim ran us through their biographies, affiliations, connections to Voron... No joke, I felt like we were in an episode of *The Sopranos*, getting ready to go to a mob war.

"And these three are here in Chattanooga?" I asked as Tim finally wrapped up his dissertation. "And they've been seen in the Sorbonne?"

"Yes, that's what we heard," Ronnie said.

"I'm tracing their cells now, live," Tim said. "Okay,

they're in a hotel at Hamilton Place, all in one room. What the heck are they doing here?"

"Great," I muttered. First Voron, and now his friends? I couldn't wait to meet them.

"Great?" Ronnie asked, then without waiting for an answer, said, "Not great at all. Surely you're not thinking of going in there?"

"Of course not. Why would I meet them on their own turf? No, Ronnie, I'm going to play with them on my turf."

"The Sorbonne?"

"Damn right. I'll call the Sorbonne and have them let us know when the trio shows up at the bar. Probably a good idea to ask Laura."

"You think?" Ronnie said with a smile.

I've always gotten along well with Laura, Benny Hinkle's business partner and premiere asset. She's the quintessential Southern barkeep: a bottle blond in a tank top one size too small, cut-off jean shorts, cowboy boots, and an exaggerated southern drawl she drops as soon as she walks out of the door.

She answered her phone after just two rings.

I explained the situation to her and asked her to be on the lookout for our deadly trio—though I didn't use the word deadly—and to call me the minute they showed up.

"Laura is on board," I said. "She says they've been in almost every night for the last week."

"If I were you," Ronnie said, "I'd let Kate know. It's kinda important, and it's her case."

I agreed with that last bit. I nodded and said, "If I know Kate, which I do, Ronnie, she's already all over it."

He shrugged. "If you say so, Harry."

"That I do, my friend; that I do."

I sat back in my chair, stared at my now empty coffee cup, then at Jacque. She tilted her head, quizzically.

"You getting all this?" I asked.

"Of course I am."

I can't tell you I was out of my depth; I wasn't, but I wasn't used to going it alone, and by alone, I mean without the support and resources of the police department. I no longer had a boss, which was good, but there were no longer colleagues with whom I could brainstorm. Yes, I had my new crew... "new" being the operative word. They were all new to law enforcement. I didn't even have Kate...

I'm going to have to call her and bring her into the loop.

I shook my head, stopped daydreaming, and made a decision.

"Tim, I have another job for you."

His eyes lit up. He was hungry and always ready to jump at an opportunity to test his skills and hack into some new database or system. Part of me wondered if enabling him wasn't a mistake, but I persuaded myself it was all for a good cause and, so long as we didn't abuse... Will you listen to me making excuses? It was wrong and I was going to have to put a stop to it, but not that day.

I really must get around to it... one of these days.

"Can you hack into a private CCTV feed?" I asked.

"Of course."

Of course, I repeated in my head. Aloud, I said, "Here's Jim McDowell's address. There's one of those security tags at the front gate. You know what I'm talking about, right? States the place is protected by Max 10 Security Concepts. I need security footage for the last, let's say, two weeks."

That should be long enough to catch Jim's mystery guest.

"Consider it done, Harry," he replied. "Before I do though, is there anything else you'd like to know about these guys?" He gestured at the flat screen. "Uh-oh, they are on the move."

"Just keep tabs on them for now, Tim, at least until I find out what the hell they're doing in my city."

He nodded and began tapping at the keyboard. I turned to talk to Jacque, but before I could open my mouth to speak, Tim looked up from his laptop.

"I'm in," he said with a smirk on his face.

"In where?" Ronnie asked.

"Max 10's servers. I'm downloading the footage now."

Holy crap... Is it that frickin' easy? I need to get him to check out my own system.

We spent the next three hours scanning through two weeks' worth of security footage from Jim McDowell's mansion on the big screen. At the end of the third hour, Ronnie's eyes were watering, and even Tim looked less than inspired... and then, we caught a break.

"There, look, see?" I said, pointing at the TV.

Tim paused the footage. A car had stopped at the iron gate, and a woman had stepped out. *Uber or Lyft maybe? Hmmm.*

"Play it," I said.

Tim clicked on his computer.

She stepped to the speaker box, tapped a button, leaned in close, said something, and the gate began to open. She turned again and reentered the back seat of the car which drove on slowly through the gate.

She was wearing jeans and some sort of baggy, colored blouse. Her blond hair was cropped short, and she was wearing sunglasses that hid almost half of her face, which made it difficult to judge her age. But from the way she moved, I figured she must be quite a lot younger than Jim McDowell... but she did not look like the type of woman

District Court Judge McDowell would have an affair with.

Then again, what the hell do I know?

"That's her," I said. "It must be. Can you pull more footage?"

He bobbed his head sideways, back and forth, like one of those bobbleheads, then said, "Maybe. I'll grab as much as they have stored on their servers. Might not be easy, though. Sometimes it auto-erases after a period, or compresses it, which might take extra time to—"

"Just do what you do, Tim," I interrupted him. "Look through as much of it as you can and find me a decent image of her, then see if you can find her for me. Okay?"

"Yessir."

"Good. Do you think you'll be able to ID her from the footage?" I asked.

Tim said, "Sure. I can create a photo composite out of every frame we have of her face, and then run it through the FBI face-recog' software."

Holy cow!

"The FBI, Tim? That's not... Oh, to hell with it. Good thinking, Tim. If she's ever been in the system, we'll know her whole life story. Very good. Just be careful you don't get caught."

He cut me a look that said it all, "as if!"

Ronnie's phone beeped. He read the message and passed it to me. It was from Laura: *Your boys are in the house.*

"Showtime," I said, getting up. To Tim, I said, "They're at the Sorbonne. Can you confirm?"

He tapped the keys, and the screenshot changed to a map.

"Yes, all three are there."

"Not the brightest bunch, huh?" Ronnie said.

"We'll see soon enough," I said, shoving my seat back as I stood up.

Out of habit, I put my hand to my right hip, where my M&P rested snugly in its holster. *Twelve in the mag and one in the chamber. Good. Plenty to go around if things go sideways, which they do more often than not.*

I thought about calling Kate, maybe go in together, like the good old days, but Kate was still a cop, and would be bound to take charge, which was not what I wanted. Even so, I would have felt better if I'd had back-up, but Ronnie and Tim weren't up to that. I needed to keep them well away from any potentially dangerous action.

"Right, then," I said. "I'm gone. Wish me luck."

"Be careful, Harry," Jacque said.

"Good luck," Tim said.

Ronnie saluted with two fingers.

I drove below the speed limit, almost in a meditative state of mind, thinking about what I had to do. My plan, if you could call it that, was simply to try to engage them in conversation, and then maybe push them a little, see if I could get them to talk, give me a little something I could work with.

True, the Sorbonne was my home turf, but that didn't mean I was safe there. If things were to get out of hand, would Laura come running to save my ass? I doubted it. Benny Hinkle? Nah, he'd keep his distance, watch, and then commiserate; not that I'd blame him... well, not hardly.

So, I would hope for the best, plan for the worst.

I had to smile as I pulled in at the curb on Prospect, a quiet service street at the rear of the Sorbonne. Remember when I said Kate would be all over the Russian hitmen? Well...

I killed the engine, stepped out, and walked across the street to a parked car and knocked on the driver-side window. Kate looked up at me, then rolled it down.

"Beat you to it?" she said.

"It isn't a competition, Kate," I said with mock serious-ness, then circled the car and got in beside her. "Show me yours, I'll show you mine?" I asked playfully.

But Kate was all cop and no play.

We spent the next few minutes exchanging intel about the troublesome trio inside the bar, which meant I was doing the giving and Kate was doing the receiving. There was only so much the CPD had access to, and they didn't have a Tim Clarke.

"And you know all of this how?" Kate asked.

I grinned. "You don't want to know, trust me."

She shook her head. "You watch your ass, Harry Starke. Be careful, okay? This is getting serious."

"It's always been serious for me, you know that."

"That's not what I meant, butthead. I don't want you to get in trouble, Harry. Or worse."

I put my hand on hers. "That's why I have you, my little peach. And this little guy." I patted my hip. "By the way, why are you alone?"

"They're on their way," she said, rolling her eyes. "I was actually waiting for them when you showed up."

"Good. Can I ask you something? Could you wait for them a while longer? I have a feeling these three guys are not into sharing drinks with cops."

"I can't promise you anything, but I'll stall." She checked her wristwatch. "You have maybe twenty, maybe thirty minutes."

"I'd better go on in, then," I said, and then, "I miss this, Kate, you and me, just the two of us on a stakeout."

"Yeah. Feels good, doesn't it?" she asked dryly. "Look, you want some time alone with these guys, you better move it, Harry."

She was right. I got out of her car, tapped twice on the roof, gave her a thumbs-up, and walked across the street and into the Sorbonne via the rear door.

9

I made my way along the dark passageway, past the restrooms, and into the bar. As per usual, the place was loud, stinky, and full of drunks... well, semi-drunks, most of them.

I found an empty stool at the bar and sat down, trying not to attract attention.

I spun on my seat, first one way then the other: the three men I was looking for were in a corner booth, exactly the one I would've chosen myself. It had easy access to the rear passageway, the restrooms, and the rear exit.

Smart? Maybe, maybe not. Maybe it was the only available booth. I couldn't know for sure, but I couldn't underestimate them, either. Discreetly, I gave them the once-over. They were all in their late sixties, drinking beer, vodka, and laughing, not a care in the world. Deceptive. Their tattooed wrists gave them away, to me anyway. To anyone else, they were a trio of retirees out for a quiet drink, nothing more...

Could they really have carried out a revenge killing?

I spun the stool back to face the bar; Laura was there, ready to take an order. She looked good in a red flannel shirt with a white tank top underneath, and I'm sure the amount of cleavage on display was bringing in the tips even this early in the evening.

"What's going on, Harry?" she said, wiping out a pint glass.

"Hey, Laura. Not much. How are you?"

"Good... Be back in a mo'." And she hurried away to the other end of the bar to refill someone's wine glass and deliver more shots.

I exhaled deeply and looked into the mirror behind the liquor shelves. To my right was a group of college kids, either med or engineering students, judging by the bags under their eyes. They laughed and drank and joked and talked nonsense.

At least they're having a good time.

Just to my left was a couple—a sleazy-looking guy in a business suit and a girl who looked like a hooker but was obviously too into the guy's lame story to actually be one.

Next to them sat a lonely dude with a small glass of what passed for whiskey at Chez Hinkle. He was a big guy, two-thirty, maybe two-forty pounds, most of it muscle, obviously military, or ex-military, like a lot of guys I knew. I watched as he took a sip of his drink, then put the glass down and looked up, straight at me through the mirror. I held his gaze, then frowned at him, but he merely smirked, shook his head like I was stupid or something, then looked away and took another sip.

What's with that guy? I wondered. Any other night I might have gotten up and asked him, but I was on a mission. And then, thankfully, Laura reappeared with my usual shot of scotch and a glass of beer.

"Anything else?" she said.

"Oh, I don't know. I'll have the lobster with a green salad on the side," I said playfully.

"Screw you, Harry," Laura smiled.

"So, what can you tell me about those three?" I made a small motion with my head in the direction of the booth in the corner.

"Well, they're nice gentlemen, actually." Which was code for good tippers. "They speak Russian or something, so I've no idea what the hell they're talking about. They're drinking beer and vodka; holding it well, too."

"Right. Okay, well that's something, I suppose." I gave her fifty bucks for the drinks and the tip-off and should've probably given more, considering the kind of crooks she'd been keeping her eye on.

"Anything else?" she asked.

"No lobster and salad, then?"

"Harry, you better hope those three find you as funny as I do." She didn't smile, but I knew it was said in jest.

I downed my whiskey and took two big gulps of beer, because time was of the essence. The big guy in the mirror gave me a sharp look, but I decided he was of no account.

I took the beer glass—half-full—with me, not just to appear casual; it would make a handy weapon, should I need it.

"Evening, guys." I would've been loud as I said it, had it not been for the loud music in the joint.

The three hitmen looked up at me, and one of them, whom I identified as Paper Boy, glanced at my hip, and then at his buddies. Was I busted already? I didn't think so; I had my hand in my pants pocket hiding the slight bulge of the M&P9 hidden under my untucked shirt.

The other two, Tesak and Brick, smirked at each other,

and then Brick said, in an accent thicker than Voron's, "You are Harry Starke, yes?"

Brick had the physique of an ex-bodybuilder—broad-shouldered and stocky. He took up most of his side of the table.

"I'm Starke, yes."

"Please, sit, Harry Starke," Tesak said, his accent almost as thick as Brick's, who did his best to scoot over.

I sat down. Sipped my beer, and made eye contact, one after the other, with all three, and it wasn't easy with the big man sitting to my left.

Voron had obviously tipped them off, but I wasn't about to let that derail my plans.

"So. You know why I'm here, then," I said.

Tesak said, "Sandra McDowell, she's died." He raised his beer glass, and the others followed suit.

They looked at me, waiting to join them.

"Sandra McDowell was murdered," I said and took a drink.

"Vlad told us so, yes. A great tragedy. *Mir yey pukhom.*"

"What?" I asked.

"God rest her soul," Paper Boy translated.

They drank again, but I didn't.

"You... any of you, d'you have any thoughts about it?"

I felt Brick shrug next to me.

Paper Boy said, "Sandra was wonderful woman. Good wife, good mother." The other two nodded, sagely. "You make progress in your investigation, da?"

I'm about to, you asshole, I thought. Instead, I said, "That's why I'm here. Where were you that night?"

Tesak sighed and said, "We are old men, Mr. Starke. I will be seventy next autumn. Our days of running around at night and getting in trouble, they are long past. We were at our hotel, sleeping."

"And I'm sure the clerk at your hotel can confirm that," I said.

"The clerk, cameras, GPS on our cell phones..."

Paper Boy reached for his pocket, and I tensed... and then relaxed again.

He took out his phone. "I have fitness program here, you see?" He held it so that I could see it. "It reads my location and counts steps. Is very useful, I like it. Here, see?"

He showed me the program, and it did seem to confirm their words. Then again, how hard would it be to fake something like that? For all I knew, Paper Boy left his phone home the night they killed Sandra.

"Mr. Starke," Brick said.

I turned to the man awkwardly. "Yes?"

"We are in Tennessee for a week, to see our old friend before he... To say our goodbyes. You understand, da?"

"That's nice of you, Brick, except Voron is in Nashville, and this is Chattanooga. You're about a hundred and sixty miles off. What gives?"

Tesak said, "We had to stay somewhere. We heard your town was beautiful this time of year, did we not?"

The other two nodded.

I was beginning to get tired of the old bastards and their over-friendly act. They were cold-blooded killers, all three of them. They didn't do friendly... ev-er. Why were they putting on an act for me? Was it boys' night out at the nursing home? Were they really old friends visiting Chattanooga for the scenery? My head was spinning with questions.

"So," I said, "you said hello to Voron and then decided to fly to Chattanooga because you've heard of our fine tourist attractions, huh? And you just happened to be in town when Sandra McDowell, the wife of Judge McDowell, who just happened to give Voron his voucher for a lethal injection, was beaten to death with a tire iron?"

The three aging assassins exchanged looks, and I stopped rambling and stared around the table, waiting... for what, I had no idea.

Paper Boy looked at me through half-closed eyes and said, "Is that damn school..."

"What? What did you say?"

"Sandra worked at school," Brick said.

Tesak gave his companions unhappy looks. He said, "Listen, Harry Starke, this is none of our business. We are here as tourists, to see America. If you don't mind—"

"Oh, I do mind," I said. "I'm done playing your mind games, Tesak. If you've got something to say, say it."

The killers chuckled.

Paper Boy said, "Mr. Starke, we've been playing these games since before you were born."

Tesak raised a hand. "Between us, Harry Starke?"

"Sure."

"Hypothetically—is a good word, no?—let us say Voron has some old war buddies, eh? And when he went away, he asked them to look after a certain judge he knew and his lovely wife..."

"What? You're not frickin' serious?" I said.

"Serious? Yes! Voron's friends are good friends and good at what they do. So they look after the judge and his wife, and they found out a lot about where she works and who she sees, works with. Maybeee..." he drew the word out, nodding his head from side to side, "just maybe, they even saw her at the school where she sometimes works. And they

thought that school was one sketchy—is that how you say it?
—place to work."

"Yeah, and yeah?" I said.

Sketchy? What the hell does he mean by that? And why were they looking after the judge and his wife? Am I misreading it? They're full o' crap, got to be, for sure!

"Oh, yeah," Paper Boy agreed.

Tesak said, "And Voron's friends would know a sketchy workplace, Mr. Starke, because they are Voron's friends."

"Hypothetically?" I asked.

Tesak only shrugged, but I sensed confirmation.

"You didn't do such a good job then, did you? Sandra's dead, which means either you screwed up or you killed her."

"Regretfully," Tesak said, "we—as you say—screwed up; that is true. We are getting old, my angry friend."

I didn't believe a word of it, but... "What's so sketchy about that school, anyway?" I asked. "The cops didn't find anything suspicious there."

The hitmen laughed, then drank to that.

Brick said, "Cops? Ha!"

"I need an answer," I insisted, and lifted the hem of my shirt to make the point.

Tesak and Paper Boy glanced at the butt of my Smith & Wesson with little interest, and Brick ignored my gesture completely.

Tesak said, "Cover it up, Mr. Starke. You don't need it here. Go to that school and look for yourself. You are a detective, yes? So you know what to do! Now, we have entertained you long enough. Now it is time for us to drink to our old friend, to celebrate good times, better times, and then go to our hotel to rest."

I considered my options and realized there weren't too

many. What was I going to do? Pull out my gun in the middle of a crowded bar and point it at the old guys? I had no way of knowing whether the lead Tesak had just given me was legit or just a quick and clunky lie to get me out of their hair, what little they had left of it.

In the end, I let the hem of my shirt fall back into place and leaned back in my seat. Any minute now I expected Kate to walk through the front door with half the CPD behind her.

"Gentlemen," I said, "I appreciate your cooperation."

"*Na Zdorovie,*" Tesak replied.

They all three drank as I got up and walked away.

Wow, those old bastards can sure put it away, the drink.

The couple was no longer at the bar, and the college crowd had thinned, but the big ex-military dude was still there, nursing the same glass of scotch, and he was staring at me.

Has he drunk any of it at all? I wondered as I walked up to the guy and stood there, in his personal space, waiting.

He looked at me through the mirror and then turned to face me.

"You need help, buddy?" he asked, staring at me.

"Looks like you're the one who needs help, *buddy*. You got a problem with me? Speak up."

He shrugged. "No problem, man, just trying to enjoy my drink. How about yourself? Can I buy you one?"

"I—" I didn't get a chance to finish.

The front door flew open and a half-dozen uniformed police officers stormed in, guns drawn and ready to shoot.

"Police!" one of them yelled, a sergeant who looked kind of familiar. "Nobody move! Kill the music, now! I said now!"

Out of the corner of my eye, I saw Laura turn off the

stereo. I turned quickly, my back to the bar, my hands where they could see them, and watched the officers spread out, handguns raised. Before the sergeant could shout his next order, a gunshot shattered the unnatural silence inside the small space, and one of the officers spun around and dropped to the floor.

"Get down!" the ex-military guy at the bar shouted. "Down!"

Instinctively, I dropped to my knees and jerked my gun from its holster—not a smart thing to do in front of a half-dozen armed and freaked-out cops.

"On your right," the guy said, clutching his glass—now empty of whiskey—like a hand grenade.

Brick and Paper Boy were on their feet, small revolvers in their hands—they glittered under the black lights—and they both were shooting; the noise inside that bar was earsplitting.

The big guy launched his glass like a damn baseball player. It spun through the air, sparkling like a diamond, and then slammed into Brick's wrist, knocking the revolver out of his hand. The huge man let out a growl and dropped into a low crouch.

I fired a single shot and, as I would learn later, I managed to clip Paper Boy's shoulder—not like me at all, but in the moment, in all the confusion... Unfortunately for him, though, the CPD was returning fire, and the old man went down, hard, hitting his head on the edge of the table.

Tesak, seeing both of his companions down, yelled something in Russian at Brick, then made a run for the passageway and the rear exit.

Brick waved a hand at him, crouched down behind the booth, and then he too ran for the rear exit. I started after him, staying low, out of sight of the jumpy cops.

Wait! I slowed, stopped for a second, my mind racing. *Where the hell's Kate? Damn, she must still be out back.*

"Cease fire!" the sergeant shouted.

And suddenly the silence hit the room like a thunderclap; it was palpable, solid, like a blanket, so thick you could almost touch it. Nobody was moving; it was frickin' unnerving. My ears were ringing. I took a breath and then, staying low, I followed Brick into the passageway. It was clear; the rear exit door was slowly closing.

As I ran down the passageway, I heard shots outside and then tires squealing. I hit the door hard with my right hip, burst through, out into the cold night air, my gun in both hands, raised, ready.

The two Russians were gone. I saw the rear end of the big car fishtail as it made the turn onto 5th and the driver hit the gas. I heard the tires squealing as they made the turn onto Market Street, which way, I had no idea, nor did I care. Across the street, a uniformed officer was on the ground next to a police cruiser... in a pool of blood... and next to him...

Oh, my God, no... Kate!

10

"K ate!" I yelled as I sprinted across the street. More people were spilling out of the door behind me, shouting, but I didn't care. My eyes were fixed on Kate, lying on the ground, hand on her chest.

I jammed my gun into its holster and knelt down beside her. Thankfully, she was conscious, as was the officer lying next to her. *I know him... Florez.*

"Kate?" I said, taking her hand.

"I'm fine," she said coughing, "fine. See?"

She struggled up onto one elbow and pointed at her bulletproof vest. A deformed bullet was nested in a hole right in the center of her chest, right where her sternum would be.

Officer Florez wasn't as lucky. He'd taken a hit to the shoulder, just below his armpit. The bullet must've gone all the way through, and he was bleeding profusely. Florez was in big trouble. He clenched his teeth, shut his eyes, the back of his head on the concrete.

"We need help here, fast!" I yelled, looking around.

"Sergeant, call for an ambulance and tell 'em to get here, *now!*"

He made the call on his radio. His officers cleared Prospect Street and taped it off.

I turned back to Florez and applied pressure to his wound. *Damn, there's a lot of blood.*

"Sergeant," I shouted, "get over here and gimme a little help, will you?"

"I know you," the sergeant said, kneeling down beside me. "You're Harry Starke. I'm Russo. Nice to meet ya. Here, let me do that."

I let him. I rose, turned, and helped Kate to her feet. She cupped the bullet and bagged it.

"What the hell happened in there, Russo?" she demanded, frowning.

"The assholes opened fire on us, is what," he said.

"No shit!" Kate snarled.

"We barely had time to return fire before they fled."

"He's right," I said.

I didn't know Russo, but I'd been where he was—a raid gone sideways, people hurt, maybe dead—and I felt for the guy.

"I was there, Kate," I said. "Those psychos started shooting with no warning."

"Ugh." Kate rubbed her forehead. "What kind of car was that? Some old land-yacht?"

"A Mercedes 500, from the eighties. August had a similar one when I was a kid," I said. "Tinted windows."

"Right," Kate said. "Put out a BOLO on the vehicle, along with an APB on the three suspects."

I corrected her, "Two suspects."

Kate glanced at me, then at Russo, then back at me.

"You've got to be kidding me!" She headed for the emergency exit.

The Sorbonne was empty. The patrons, most of them detained outside for questioning. I didn't know whom I felt worse for, the poor drunks who'd been out for a night of partying, or the officers who had to deal with them.

"Which one is this?" Kate asked as we stood over the body.

"Paper Boy," I said. "Alexey Presnov, I think."

I looked at the old man sprawled on the floor, riddled with bullet holes, his face contorted, head twisted unnaturally; he'd been hit at least six times that I could see.

"One down, two to go," I said quietly.

Kate crouched down, reached under the table and picked up the man's revolver, holding it with two fingers by the barrel.

"Bag, please," she called, and a moment later, an officer bagged the gun.

We sat at the bar then, and I told Kate my version of what had gone down. She wasn't happy, and neither was Assistant Chief Henry Finkle when he arrived twenty minutes later.

He stalked in through the front door with fire in his eyes, stopped, looked around, then walked to the body, stood over it for a moment, then stepped up to the bar. He was Kate's boss, and he wasn't happy to see me seated next to her.

"You?" he snarled. "What the hell are you doing here, Starke? This is a crime scene, and you've no business here."

I smiled benignly at him and said, "To be fair, Henry, I *was* here first."

Finkle wasn't amused. "And why is that, exactly? Was this your doing?" He gestured at Paper Boy's body.

"Nah, that was one of your boys, Henry. I'm simply a bystander, a concerned citizen, you might say."

"Concerned my ass," Finkle said.

"Sir," Kate said, "Harry happened to be here when the raid took place. There was no way he could've known."

Finkle squinted his eyes at both of us, and I shrugged.

"What can I say, I like the vibes here, though not so much tonight, but—"

"Enough, Starke! Give your statement and get the hell out of my sight."

"I'll look after that, sir, later," Kate said.

He cut her a look that would have frozen a waterfall.

Sergeant Russo joined us with his radio still in his hand. "They've found the car. They set it on fire about five miles west of here, in a lane off Wauhatchie Pike. The Fire Department is on it."

"Hey, Russo," I said. "How's Florez? And what happened to the officer I saw get hit in here?"

"Florez'll make it. The EMTs are loading him up now. Officer Tate took one to the vest, small caliber—thirty-two, I think. He's fine."

"Florez?" Finkle asked. "EMTs? What the hell happened?"

"He took one in the shoulder, Chief," Russo said. "He lost some blood, but they don't seem to be too concerned."

"You taped off the area, right?" Kate asked, knowing good and well that he had, but saying it for Finkle's benefit anyway.

Russo nodded.

"Good," she said. "Get Mike Willis and his CSI team down here, ASAP. Maybe we'll get lucky."

Russo looked at Finkle, who gave him a nod and snapped, "Well, get on with it, Russo!"

Russo hurried away, and Finkle looked at Kate, saw the hole in her vest.

"Are you hurt, Sergeant Gazzara?" he said.

"I'm okay. Could use some rest though."

"You sure you don't need to go to the hospital?"

"I'm fine," Kate insisted.

"Very well, then. Take the rest of the night off but keep your phone within reach."

"Will do, sir."

Back at her car, Kate took off the bulletproof vest and put it in the trunk. I could see she was in pain.

"Could you give me a lift home?" she asked.

"How about I give you a lift to my place?" I said.

"Do you have some of that good scotch you like to drink?"

I looked at her. "Are you serious? Always! Let's go."

A half an hour later, Kate was seated on the couch in my living room and I was pouring her a scotch. I handed it to her, poured one for myself, and sat down opposite her.

I was worried about her. I'd already come off my adrenaline rush, but she was quiet. I hoped the drink would help calm her nerves. You don't get over being shot in a hurry, even if you're wearing a vest. Your first reaction is a rush of relief, your second is shock, and then the enormity of it, and how things might have been, sinks in. No! You don't get over it in a hurry.

Kate took a big sip of the scotch. "Ah, this is nice," she said, her eyes closed.

"Nice?" I said as I sipped mine. "Laphroaig is not nice, it's exquisite. How're you feeling?"

She touched two fingers to her chest. I put my glass down, stepped over to her, kneeled down in front of her and undid the top button of her shirt, and then two more. I opened her blouse. There was a large, dark bruise between her breasts, just above the bridge of her bra. I touched it gently.

"Ou-ch."

"Sorry. That's going to hurt for a while."

She finished her scotch in two big gulps and put the empty glass down.

"It seems," she said, "that once again we find ourselves in a *touchy* situation."

"I know. I'm sorry, but touching you..." I put a hand on her waist. "How about here?"

She nodded.

I moved my hand. "Here?"

She nodded again, put her hands on my shoulders, leaned in, and kissed me.

"I got shot, Harry," she whispered. "I got freakin' shot. It scared me."

I stood, took both her hands in mine. "I know... Come on, you need a hot shower. Then I'll rub some of that blue ibuprofen crap on it. It will help."

She stood, wrapped her arms around my neck, kissed me, leaned back, looked deep into my eyes, and said, "The shower sounds good, but the blue stuff... That's not what I need, Harry. You can do better."

And I did.

11

The next morning, I woke before my alarm went off. Kate turned over in the bed beside me, and I could see that the bruise on her chest had darkened. The early morning sun played on her skin and her blond hair, and I couldn't help myself but kiss her.

"Morning, Harry," she mumbled. "What time is it?"

"About ten minutes before the alarm," I replied.

"Good," she said and closed her eyes.

She smiled when I kissed her again, and I slipped out of bed. There were two missed calls and a text from Tim on my iPhone, and I opened the message on my way to the shower.

I saw a photograph of a pretty young woman. Perfect face, full lips slightly raised in the corners, light blue eyes, short blond hair. She could've been an actress or a model, but the description underneath mentioned neither.

Her name was Mary Turner, and she was 26 years old, a Chattanooga native. Both parents deceased. She never married but had a five-year-old daughter, Penny Turner.

There was an address, and I made a note to pay Mary a visit later in the day. That done, I showered and brewed some coffee.

My head was giving me trouble. I might have felt like a twenty-year-old, but my body knew I was thirty-six, and the whiskey, not to mention the close proximity to gunfire in an enclosed space, had given me a mild headache. I drank some coffee and almost shivered with pleasure. Sometimes simple things were that good.

Kate came out of the bedroom, yawning, running her hands through her hair, wearing nothing but her panties and one of my shirts with most of the buttons undone. I handed her a cup.

"Good morning, gorgeous," I said, but saw that Kate was already becoming her cop self again.

She smiled warmly, but said, "You never told me what you learned from the Russians."

I nodded. I hadn't.

"Pretty much the same BS I learned from Voron," I said.

"Pretty much, Harry?" she said with a thin smile.

"Okay, okay, I may have something. Tesak, the smaller dude of the two that got away—"

"The bastard who shot me. Continue, please." Kate sipped her coffee.

I shook my head. "Yeah, that one. He told me there's something up with that school Sandra's daughter goes to. The one you said you checked out."

She frowned, wrinkled her nose, then said, "Yeah, we checked it out. But come on, Harry, it's Belle Edmondson, for Pete's sake. The dang place is as old as the city and people fight to get in. There's nothing out of the ordinary going on up there; it's just a school, a very good, very expensive school... Did he say anything else, this Tesak? I can't request a warrant to search the place because some Russian killer doesn't like it."

"Thankfully, I don't need a warrant, Kate. In your estimation, who's the guy at the school that's most likely to crack... under pressure?" I held my breath. Kate doesn't like it when I talk pressure.

I didn't exactly have a plan at that moment, but my mind was racing. We had at least three avenues we could pursue: the school, the blond girl Mary Turner, and the two escaped elderly assassins, who couldn't stay hidden for long.

Kate played with her hair, thinking. Then, she said, "There's this one guy, Robert Rainer. He seemed kind of weird... withdrawn maybe... when I questioned him."

"Weird how?" I asked.

"I had the feeling he wasn't telling me everything he knew about the board meeting the night Sandra was killed. I kind of got the idea that something had happened, just before she left to go home, but I couldn't get anything out of anyone who was there that night."

"Gotcha, I can work with that." I grinned. "Robert Rainer, huh? I'll see what I can do."

"Work your magic, Harry, but for Pete's sake don't cause any trouble up there... or hurt anyone. We don't want another situation like we had at the Sorbonne."

I raised my hands in defense. "That wasn't me."

"I know, but I'm the one who has to deal with the fallout." She set her cup down. "Speaking of which, I need to get going. Thanks." She kissed me lightly.

"For last night?" I asked, smiling.

"For the coffee." She winked and headed into the bedroom.

Five minutes later she stepped out again, all cop, no lover.

"Do you want to join me on my visit to the school?" I said.

"You know I can't, not after last night's fiasco. And I just received a text from Finkle. I have a mandatory psych evaluation in half an hour, so... and then there's the writing and reading reports." She heaved a huge sigh, shook her head. "I gotta go, Harry."

I gave her a ride to The Sorbonne, where she'd left her car the previous night. The place was closed and taped off, a blue and white cruiser with two uniforms inside was parked behind Kate's car. She had a quick word with the driver, turned and waved at me, then got into her car and drove away. Me? I headed for the Belle Edmondson prep school, on Signal Mountain.

I felt a little guilty in that I hadn't told her about the possibility that Jim McDowell might be having an affair. But I had a good excuse: I wanted to be sure before I ruined his life, reputation, and career. I also kept Mary Turner to myself, again until I knew exactly what the connection was... or wasn't.

It was a pleasant drive to Belle Edmondson. I was impatient, but I drove at my leisure and even turned on the radio and listened to some music, until it was interrupted by the news: *"A riot has broken out at a Nashville prison this morning, when a number of inmates started a fight during breakfast. The riot quickly spread until the entire prison was involved. At least two guards were injured and are being treated at Vanderbilt University Hospital. Tensions at the prison have been running high at the Riverbend Maximum Security Institute since the date and time of the execution of Vladislav Voronov, the notorious Russian assassin was announced. We will, of course, keep you updated as the situation continues to evolve. In other news...*

I shook my head. *You win this one, Voron, whatever it is you're up to,* I thought, and I switched the station.

A pre-Civil War military academy, the Belle Edmondson complex is a grandiose collection of stone-built, crenelated structures now an intimidatingly expensive all-girls preparatory school, eight through twelfth grades with the option to stay on for a year of college prep and an almost guaranteed spot in one of the Ivy League universities. The students come from all over the world, and there are always more applicants than there are spots. You get accepted at Belle Edmondson, and you're set for life.

I parked in the visitor section of the lot and climbed the steps to the administration building. The inside of the place was just as grandiose as the exterior, and expensive: wood, marble, and a lot of light. The walls of the hallway were decorated with golden-framed portraits of notable graduates, mostly politicians and entrepreneurs, all girls of course, in identical black dresses, though there was one girl I took to be some sort of a pop star, with colorful hair and a shiny yellow jacket.

Good for you, girlfriend, I thought.

To my left, a girl aged about eighteen was seated on a bench at the wall listening to her iPhone. I recognized her immediately. It was Chelsea McDowell.

"Hey, Chelsea?" I said.

She looked up at me and rolled her eyes—teenagers—and took out an earbud and said, "Come again?"

"Hi, Chelsea. I'm Harry Starke."

"Good for you," she replied.

She was frustrated, and I knew why, so I took no offense.

"What are you doing here, at school?" I said.

In retrospect, it wasn't the best question to ask her at that particular moment.

"Huh?" She half-closed her eyes and wrinkled her nose.

I said, "Never mind. Listen, do you know where I can find Robert Rainer?"

"Who did you say you are?" she said. "I don't know you. I can scream, you know. They don't like creeps hanging out around here; it's a girls' school."

"Cool it, Chelsea. I'm working for your father," I said, holding up my hands palms-out. "And I need to speak to Robert Rainer?"

"Oh, Bobby Rain?" She giggled. "Bobby's a dickhead. He dwells in the admin offices. Down the hallway on your right."

"Thanks," I said, gifting her with a smile.

She just rolled her eyes again, shook her head in mock disgust, stuffed the bud back in her ear, and went back to browsing on her phone.

Kids... Geez, who wants 'em?

I found the Administration Offices, just as she said, down the hallway on my right. I knocked on the door and stepped inside a huge, empty room: there were five desks, all with computers, lock screens lit, but no people.

I stood in the doorway for a moment, and then walked across the room to a door that read "Robert Rainer, Hamilton County School Board Liaison." I knocked.

"Come in."

I opened the door, stepped inside, and said, "Mr. Rainer?"

"That would be me," he replied, rising to his feet.

Rainer was a thin guy in his early thirties, but he could easily have passed for a student. Well, no, not really; he didn't look like a girl, he... Ah, forget it. He was wearing a navy pullover, button-down shirt and tie, with navy pants. He looked at me through thin-rimmed glasses, confused.

"May I help you, Mister..." he asked.

"I hope so, Mr. Rainer. My name's Harry Starke. I'm a private investigator."

He gave me a weak handshake.

I said, "Judge McDowell hired me to look into his wife's murder."

Rainer looked aside. *And there's the tell. He knows something. Now to turn the screw.*

"I've already told the police—"

"I'm not with the police, Robert," I interrupted him, then continued in a what I hoped sounded like a confidential tone, "And the cops aren't too eager to share intel. The good news—for you—is I'm not eager to share with them either. I work for Sandra's husband, so that's my priority. I just want to find her killer."

Rainer sat down, and so did I. He cracked his knuckles, then licked his lips, inhaled, then exhaled.

Then he said, "I don't know what to tell you, Mr. Starke. We had a budget meeting, discussed new projects, next year's grants and such... and that was it."

I didn't respond for a long moment, waiting for him to fill the awkward silence, looking at him expectantly.

Rainer said, "Sandra loved the kids. Her daughter goes to this school, as I'm sure you know, so she was always supportive, financing scholarships and programs for the less... fortunate kids."

Less fortunate kids? Are you kidding me? You mean the ones that don't own Porsches?

I nodded. *He sounds sincere, but he's holding back...*

"Did Sandra have any problems with any members of

the faculty, or members of the School Board? Did she have any enemies?" I asked.

Rainer shook his head. "Not that I know of. Everyone enjoyed working with Sandra," he said, picking up a pen and a yellow sticky note. "Though, she did have some controversial opinions." He jotted something down. "Not everyone liked giving away money. She didn't work here, you know." He handed me the note and looked me in the eye. "But absolutely everyone loved Sandra McDowell, and she was very generous."

I glanced at the note, then said, "I see. Well, thank you for your time, Mr. Rainer. I won't take up any more of it."

"No problem," he replied, and we both stood up. "Let me know if I can help further."

"Of course."

With that, I stepped out of his office and then out into the hallway, closing the door behind me.

I stood for a moment and looked at the note: *Meet me at Cafe Del Luna, 4 PM.*

I shook my head, folded the note, slipped it into my pocket, turned and...

"Whoops, I'm sorry."

12

"And good day to you!" the woman I bumped into said. "Excuse me." Her eyes narrowed. "Who are you? Have we met?" She cocked her head, looking me over, jerkily, like an owl.

"My apologies," I said. "I should have been looking where I was going. No, ma'am. I don't believe we have met." I held out my hand. "My name's Harry Starke. I'm a private investigator. I was just talking to Mr. Rainer. I'm looking into the death of Sandra McDowell."

She took my hand and shook it, twice. "Henrietta Mason, Provost." She smiled.

"Nice to meet you, ma'am," I said.

"Likewise, Harry—it is all right if I call you Harry?"

I smiled, nodded, and said, "Of course."

"Good, and please, don't call me ma'am. Call me Henry. Everybody does, including the students," and she laughed a loud, horsey laugh.

Henry? Frickin' hell... That's too much!

"Losing Sandra," she continued, seriously, "came as a terrible shock to me, and to everyone here at Belle Edmondson. Lovely woman, lovely person. How can I help you, Harry?"

"Of course. I am sorry for your loss, Henrietta. As I mentioned, I spoke to Mr. Rainer, and he only had good things to say about her."

The conversation was getting awkward, so I asked the question: "May I talk to you about Sandra, Henry?" The name got tangled in my mouth. "It would, of course, be off the record."

She shrugged nonchalantly and said, "Absolutely, absolutely. Please, let's go and sit down."

We did, and we spent the next fifteen minutes or so talking about Sandra, with Henry doing most of the talking... and this is what I learned: everyone loved Sandra, and everyone mourned her loss.

Sheesh, what a waste of time.

"I appreciate your help," I said finally, rising to my feet.

"Any time, Harry, any time. I do hope the Chattanooga Police also consider their investigation a priority. Sandra was a prominent member of our community and—"

"I can assure you that the CPD is all over it," I said. In truth, the last thing I wanted was the rich and privileged complaining about law enforcement. I'd dealt with enough of that during my years on the force. "Thank you again, Henry."

We shook hands, and I left her and headed back along the hallway toward the exit; Chelsea was still seated on the bench, still deep in her phone. I sat down beside her on the edge of the bench, half-turned toward her. She didn't look up or acknowledge my existence.

I unfolded the note, read it again and again, as if I was trying to unravel some sort of mystery.

Meet me at Cafe Del Luna, 4 PM.

"What's that?" Chelsea asked. Her earphones were out, the screen of her phone black.

"Beats me," I said, and I stood up to leave, but lingered. "Hey, Chelsea, do you need anything?" I asked.

She looked up at me. There was anger, sorrow, and tears in her eyes. She blinked, pursed her lips, looked at me through watery eyes and said, "Yeah."

"Can I help?"

She shook her head—a tiny, barely perceptible motion —and a tear rolled down her cheek. "No, I don't think you can."

I nodded. "Hang in there, okay? I know how tough it can be. My mom passed when I was fifteen." I looked at the floor, my thoughts flashing back to my own mother.

"Really?" Chelsea said.

"Yes, really."

"Sucks, doesn't it?"

"Sure does, Chelsea, it sure does." I nodded.

She nodded.

"Mr. Starke?"

"Yes?"

"Do you think the police will find my mom's killer?" She looked at me doe-eyed, helpless.

My innards churned with anger and at that moment... I knew, absolutely.

"If they don't, I will, Chelsea. That's a promise." I handed her one of my cards.

"If you need me, for *anything,* you call, any time, night or day. I'll be there, that's a promise too. See you around, okay?"

"Bye, and thanks," she said, holding the card with both hands.

I walked quickly to the exit, suppressing my own urge to

shed a tear for her, and for my own mother. I'd lived without her for so long that I'd almost forgotten what it felt like to be with her, and Chelsea reminded me how tough it could be. The loneliness, the constant feeling of being lost, drifting...

But I also knew that eventually, Chelsea would heal, she would become a stronger person for it.

Hang in there, kiddo.

I stepped outside and stopped for a moment at the top of the steps to get some fresh air, and my thoughts turned to the case.

What the hell is Rainer up to? I thought. *Something's definitely going on with that guy... Is he under surveillance? He acted like his office is bugged, that's for sure. Otherwise, why the note? And if the guy is afraid to speak about... whatever it is they're hiding, then it must be serious.*

And that brought the school, or, more likely, its administration, to the top of my list of suspects.

Maybe Tesak was right. Hmmm... and what the hell have Tesak and his cronies been up to all these years? And what did he mean, "look after them"?

I sighed, shook my head, and walked down the steps to my car. My phone buzzed in my pants pocket. Tim had texted Mary Turner's address. It wasn't on the way to the office, which was where I was headed after I left Belle Edmondson, but where Ms. Turner lived wasn't that much of a detour, ten minutes at most.

13

Mary Turner lived in a two-story house located in the nicer part of St. Elmo, a few blocks away from the St. Elmo Park. There wasn't a car on the short driveway in front of the house, but, if she was home, it could have been in the garage. So I parked at the curb and walked to the front door and knocked, and then I knocked again, and was just about to leave when the door opened.

"Hello?" a girl said from behind a screen door, keyword being "girl." She couldn't have been more than fifteen, with pitch-black hair, black eyeliner, and a nose piercing. She wore a leather jacket over a T-shirt that'd been washed so many times, the logo was illegible.

"Hi," I said. "I'm here to speak to Mary Turner. Is she home?"

"She's not," the girl said. "Who's asking?"

"My name's Harry Starke. I'm a private investigator."

The girl shrugged, unfazed. "Mary isn't here."

I thought I knew the answer to my next question, but I asked it anyway. "Where did she go?"

"Just to the mall."

"And you are?" I asked, and I put my hand on the door jamb.

"Kitty. I'm Mary's babysitter?"

"Ah, that's right. Can I speak with *you*, Kitty?"

She shrugged. "You are speaking with me. Also, I'm only fourteen, so..."

"I just want to ask a few questions about Mary. Somebody's been murdered and I—"

"Whoa, man," she said and almost stepped back. "Don't drop that crap on me. I've nothing to do with Mary or whatever. Now leave, go away! Or I'm gonna scream."

I stood there a moment, but then I heard a kid in the background, laughing along to some cartoon.

I grunted. "Okay, I'm sorry. Just... can you give me a call when Mary returns?"

She smirked. "No! Go!"

I did and as fast as I could.

Dammit.

Mary Turner had turned into a dead-end, at least for a while. I considered waiting in my car for her to return, but I couldn't risk the girl calling 911 on me. I knew Kate would catch up to me at some point, and that Mary would be questioned, but I'd no intention of bringing the cops in before I had to. Jim McDowell hired me to do a job, and that was my first priority.

Okay, so Mary Turner would have to wait. I fired up the engine and headed back to my office.

During the ten-minute drive to Georgia Avenue, I let my mind wander, trying to figure out the events of the previous night, mostly the shootout at the Sorbonne.

It just makes no sense. What am I missing? I have a

whole bunch of pieces to the puzzle, but I have no idea how they fit together.

Tesak, or maybe it was Brick, had told me they were in town for sightseeing, which was, of course, a joke—unbelievable. But what the hell could've caused them to open fire at first sight of the CPD? What was so important that they'd risk their lives for it, and lose one of their own in the process?

Then there was the school: another of Tesak's gems... How did he know about that? And Rainer: what was that about? I hadn't the faintest idea... and I wasn't any closer to finding out what Mary Turner was to Jim McDowell either.

What to do next? It was a puzzlement. In the end, I figured all I had, at least until something broke, was Belle Edmondson and Robert Rainer, so the first thing I did when I got back to the office, after grabbing a mug of coffee, was to ask Tim to find out all he could about the school and the people who ran it.

"Wow," Tim said as he went to work. "That's quite a place. I've heard good things. A friend's ex-girlfriend went to Edmondson. So, what do you want me to look for, exactly?" Tim turned in his chair. His battle station, now equipped with multiple monitors, system blocks and other electronic gizmos, buzzed and pinged behind him.

"Look at the faculty, primarily the administration. The President, the trustees, everyone close to the top. Run backgrounds on the staff and faculty, especially a Robert Rainer... Somebody's bugging his offices, and maybe others, and I want to know who and what we're dealing with."

I took a sip of coffee, watching as his fingers flew over the keyboard at a speed that made my head spin.

"I also want full background checks on Jim and Sandra McDowell... I want to know what she was doing with her money, especially where it concerned the school. And I need to know more about Mary Turner."

"Huh," Tim said. "The plot thickens!"

"It's too thick, if you ask me," I said. "Way too many loose ends that might not be so loose at all."

Ronnie joined us, a stack of papers in one hand and a pen in the other.

"How'd it go with the Turner girl?" he asked.

"She wasn't at home," I said.

"Yeah, we could've told you that," Ronnie said.

I looked at him for a long moment, waiting for an explanation.

"Timmo here hacked McDowell's security system, remember?"

"Yeah, and?"

Tim chimed in, "After we downloaded the back archive from the Max 10 servers, I went back in and modified their code. Added another line to the feed." He patted a small black box on this desk and said, "This little boy is keeping an eye on the house for us."

It took me a moment to process what he'd just said. "Are you telling me Mary Turner is at Jim's house right now?"

Ronnie nodded, and Tim said, "She went inside the house about two hours ago."

"Why the hell didn't you tell me? You could have saved me a very unpleasant run-in with a fourteen-year-old harpy... Okay, don't tell me," I said as Tim opened his mouth. "Let me think." I closed my eyes.

I now knew for a fact that Mary was at Jim's place and that something must be going on between them—*two hours? Come on!* But I still wasn't sure that it would be smart for me to confront them just yet. If Mary really was Jim's mistress, and they were in it together—Sandra's murder—

then I'd be walking into a nasty situation with potentially disastrous consequences. I might not be able to control the outcome of such a confrontation, and that didn't sit well with me.

On the other hand, while Kate and the rest of the CPD were tied up with the Sorbonne shootout and the dead Russian hitman, I had the rest of the day to myself. I could pick a time to go and talk to Jim without unnecessary distractions.

"Tim," I said, "I need you to keep watch on the McDowell CCTV feed for me."

Tim tapped a button, dragged a window, and one of his displays filled with a grid of different views on the McDowell's mansion. There was no sign of McDowell or Mary Turner. All seemed quiet.

"Good. Let me know if Mary or Jim leave, okay?"

Tim nodded, and I called out, "Jacque!"

She appeared a second later. "Yes, Harry?"

"Tim is going to give you and Ronnie some files to look through." I turned to Tim and said, "Give them everything you find on the Edmondson faculty, okay? The top priority is Robert Rainer." I paused, thought for a minute, then said, "Ronnie, you'll handle the financials, right?"

"Uh-huh. On it, boss."

"Will you people stop calling me that?" I said and then smiled at Ronnie's chuckle.

"Sorry, Harry," Ronnie said. "I just like to see the look on your face when we say that word."

Tim and Jacque nodded agreement, and I rolled my eyes and frowned at them jokingly.

"Okay, so everyone knows what they're doing?" I said.

"The CCTV feed and the Edmondson files," Tim said.

Ronnie said, "Yep. Jacque and I will look for anything

that stands out or doesn't add up. Where there's big money involved, there's bound to be some shenanigans."

Jacque said, "What will you do, Harry?"

"I think I'll pay a visit to Jim McDowell. It's about time we cleared a few things up. If the man's been lying to me... Well, we'll see. I'm outa here. I'll stay in touch. If Kate calls... you know nothing, you hear?"

They all nodded, and I left.

I drove fast and kept my iPhone close by, in case Tim called me with an update. If McDowell was up to something with the Turner woman, I wanted to arrive just in time to catch them at it.

My hope for that was somewhat diminished when Jim answered the intercom at the front gates.

"Hello?" he said. "Harry, is that you?"

I glanced up and saw a camera pointed at me. I stuck my head out the window and waved.

I said, "Yes, it's me, Jim."

"Didn't expect you to visit so soon. You should've called. How's the investigation going?" He didn't sound out of breath, but he did sound worried.

And I was getting annoyed by this conversation through the intercom.

I told the truth. "I might be onto something. I just wanted to give you a quick update. How about you let me in, Jim, and we can talk face-to-face like normal human beings?"

He paused and then said, "Right. Yes. Of course, come ahead, Harry."

The intercom let out a long buzz, the locks clicked, the gates opened and I drove on through and up the long, winding driveway, past stands of birch trees and perfectly trimmed hedges until I finally arrived outside the mansion. I parked behind Jim's Mercedes, walked up the steps to the front door, and thumbed the bell push. The door opened immediately and a smiling young Hispanic woman held it open and stood aside gesturing for me to enter.

I'd been to the Judge's house once before, but never long enough to admire its interior design, which I was doing when Jim descended the wide main staircase.

"Harry," he said, extending his hand. "It's so good to see you, but... well, let's go into the sitting room."

He motioned for me to sit in one of the armchairs and then sat down opposite me and lit a cigar.

"Would you like a cigar, Harry?" he asked, letting out a cloud of smoke. The way he moved told me he was merely using the stogie for something to do with his hands.

"No, thanks, Jim," I replied.

"So, why are you here? Do you have a suspect?"

"Several, actually, but nothing concrete, yet." I paused, reading the man, choosing my next words.

Did I want to outright provoke him, or chip away with leading questions? Frankly, I'd lost my patience sometime during the shootout at the Sorbonne, so I chose the former.

"Tell me about Mary Turner," I said.

His eyes widened, and smoke escaped his mouth and nostrils as if I'd punched him in the gut. The he started coughing, like he was about to throw up a lung, cleared his throat, then beat his chest with a fist.

"Mary Turner?" he gasped.

"Yes, Jim, Mary Turner. You know who I'm talking about. And I'm guessing you know that I know that she's here. Where is she?"

"What are you... What are you talking about, Harry?"

"I'm doing the job you hired me to do, Jim, and this isn't helping. If you want me to find Sandra's killer, I need to know everything so don't lie to me. Where is she and what is she to you? Are you romantically involved with her?"

Judge James McDowell, a powerful and well-respected man, turned red as a tomato as he looked at me.

"Listen, Harry, there are things that I just can't share. Not with you, not with—"

"The police?" I asked. "Judge, you know how these things go. You don't have to talk to me, but surely you realize that at some point the truth is going to come out."

"Then what difference does it make if I don't tell you now?"

I marveled at how oblivious people could get when they're cornered. Jim McDowell has been part of the system since before I was born, he should've known better.

"The difference is," I said, "that you still have control over *how* the truth comes out. Whatever goes on behind closed doors is none of my business. I don't talk to the press, and I won't talk to the police unless I absolutely have to. Your private life is yours alone, Jim, but it doesn't mean your wife's killer should go free."

He was looking down at the floor.

"Look at me, Jim. If you are having an affair, that's a strong motive for murder, and you above all people know that the spouse is always the prime suspect, until he can be eliminated, so come on. Give!"

That got to him, and he broke down. By that point, I was convinced Jim didn't murder his wife. He was in pain, back in the state he was in when we met at the Country Club a few days back. Whatever he was hiding, whoever Mary Turner really was, I believed Jim was innocent of the murder of his wife.

He put the cigar into an ashtray on the low table between us and wiped his face with a handkerchief.

"I apologize," he said.

"No need to, Jim. Just tell me the truth."

"We will," a woman's voice came from behind me.

Jim's eyes became even wider as I turned to see Mary Turner standing in the doorway with a steaming cup. The scent of Jasmine filled the air.

She looked just like the photograph Tim had created. She wore jeans and a light green shirt with the sleeves rolled up. I noticed the watch on her wrist—a Patek Philippe—and a gold chain with some sort of small ornament hanging from it. She was attractive, sure, but no great beauty, quite ordinary, in fact.

She joined us, sat down on the couch, then poured tea on Jim's cigar, filling the ashtray to the brim.

"I told you to quit smoking, didn't I?" she said, not at all intimidated by my presence. She turned to me and held her hand out. "My name is Mary Turner."

I shook her hand. "Harry Starke."

"Nice to finally meet you, Mr. Starke. Jim's told me a lot about you. Now it's time we told you about me, I suppose."

I glanced at Jim, who looked up at the ceiling and let out a heavy sigh.

"Do tell," I said, a little sarcastically.

14

"Before we start," Mary Turner said, "would you like something to drink? Tea? Coffee?"

"Scotch?" McDowell suggested.

"I'm fine, thank you," I replied. I leaned forward in my armchair, my elbows on my knees, hands clasped together in front of me.

I wasn't worried about the couple's intentions—and by "couple" I don't mean they were an item. I also knew they weren't killers—my sixth sense was telling me so—and they were projecting a strong father-daughter vibe; no sexual tension between them.

McDowell was focused on his soaked cigar, waiting for Mary to speak first, but she only looked at him.

"Well," he began. "Before we do tell you *everything*," he emphasized the word, "will you promise this will stay between us? Or at least that it won't get out for a while?"

I shook my head. "I told you I can't promise that, Jim. If I find it necessary to involve the police, I will. We're conducting a murder investigation, not some domestic dispute." I glanced at Mary. "Speaking of which. How are the two of you related, exactly? You seem to be awfully comfortable in this house, Miss Turner."

Mary cleared her throat, but my comment didn't seem to affect her confidence one bit. She said, "Yes, I am comfortable here, Mr. Starke. I've been all but living in this house almost all my life."

"Not all your life, Mary," McDowell said.

Both Mary and I gave him a look.

"Well, maybe not all my life..."

I was still looking at Jim. If he wanted to say something, I'd rather hear it from him.

Get on with it, was what I wanted to say.

What I did say was, "Why don't you start from the beginning, Jim?"

"Good idea, Harry," he said. "So, Sandra and I, we support... supported a number of charities in Chattanooga and elsewhere in Tennessee. I still support them, of course, but Sandy..." He gulped, wiped his eye with the back of his hand.

Mary leaned forward and placed a hand on his knee. "It's okay, take your time."

And he did. He asked Mary to get him a glass of water and then lit another cigar.

He watched as she left the room to get his water, then said, "Promise me you'll leave Mary out of it, Harry. She's done nothing wrong."

It was the third time he asked me to promise things I couldn't possibly agree to, so I said nothing.

"Jim," I finally said. "Don't force my hand here, all right? Talk to me, as you promised you would."

Mary returned with a glass of water and handed it to him. He drank some of it, put the glass down on the coffee table and said, "We couldn't have children, not for a long time, Sandra and me. We'd been trying since we were in our twenties, tried everything, but nothing worked."

I didn't ask for clarification.

He continued, "We became desperate, and decided we wanted to adopt a baby girl."

I turned to Mary. "And that's where you come in?"

"Yes and no," she said.

"We couldn't do it, Harry," Jim said. "We just couldn't pick a child from foster care. That would leave so many others behind, and they were all wonderful kids... you know," Jim teared up. "There are thousands of homeless, orphaned children out there, fighting for their lives every day. And we love kids, Harry. Sandy loved kids oh so much..." He picked up the glass and took another huge gulp of water, replaced it on the table and stared down at the floor.

"So you didn't adopt Mary?" I asked.

He shook his head. "Sandra and I, we founded a charity, a foundation that would provide financing for orphans in Chattanooga and all across the state. That way, instead of giving just one of those kids the lucky ticket, we figured we could help... maybe hundreds of children."

"And you have," Mary said, "and we thank you for that."

"Mary's parents passed around that time," Jim said. "It was 1988, and she'd been living in foster care for about a year. We both felt that it was time for us to commit, to adopt the child. We started working with the professionals through our organizations and... then—"

"Sandra got pregnant with Chelsea," Mary said.

There was no animus in her voice, but I didn't quite catch any sisterly love, either. I was a little confused.

"So, you were never adopted... then?" I asked.

"Not exactly," Jim said. "When we got the news of Sandra's pregnancy, we were on cloud nine, as you could imagine. It was a miracle! Naturally, Sandy focused on the future, on our baby, baby Chelsea, and stepped away from our charities for several years. But I couldn't just let her go, little Mary here." Jim smiled at Mary Turner lovingly.

"Jim?" I said, growing impatient.

"Yes, sorry. So I continued to support her. I paid for her private school, sports, tutoring, college, everything. I made sure she wanted for nothing."

"But I didn't want any of it," Mary said. "I wasn't even ten years old when I finally realized Jim and Sandra would not be adopting me. I was... disappointed, to say the least. I'd been telling the other kids about my new family, how much fun I would have, all the ice cream I'd be eating... But at some point, it became clear to me that it would not be happening."

"We didn't talk for a while after that but—"

"Not for almost ten years," Mary said, interrupting him.

"But as I said, I continued to support her," Jim said. "Chelsea was growing up, and we paid all our attention to her. She's our miracle child, but Mary always had a special place in our hearts. I knew Sandy wanted a future for both girls, so I continued financing Mary's education—a private school in Atlanta—and, well, I provided her with money through the foundation."

"I didn't want it, but I took it." Mary shrugged. "It was good money, and I needed it. I didn't go to college because by then I had a child of my own." She rubbed her eyes. "I made mistakes, okay? But when I became a mother myself..."

Jim smiled at that. "You're doing great, honey. We're so proud of you."

Mary said, "When I became a mother, I realized how tough it could be. I wanted to get together again with Jim and Sandra."

"For the money?" I asked. "You knew your sponsors were loaded, right?"

Jim twitched at my sudden dig, but if I was going to get the truth, I had to provoke them, and that meant dropping the tact. This wasn't couple's therapy and I wasn't there to take confessions.

"At first," Mary said, "yes, of course it was the money. As I said, the money was good. Penny and me, we were all alone, and I wanted the best for her too. So I thought I'd show up, guilt them into giving me some cash."

"And we delivered on the cash part, didn't we?" Jim said with a chuckle.

Mary blushed. "Yes, you did." She looked at me. "But that's not my point. Jim and Sandra, and even Chelsea, they were so happy to see us. They welcomed us into the family. I became like a long-lost cousin to the McDowells, and Penny their granddaughter. We would celebrate birthdays and go on vacations together."

For a moment, I thought what they were telling me was going to lead to another dead end. It did make sense, but not all of it, not completely.

"So," I said, "why keep it a secret? Why hide it and sneak around behind everyone's back? Why feed the rumor mill at the Country Club?"

"You said it right there," Mary said. "The Country Club. You know as well as I do that Jim and Sandra's life is... something else. Expensive cars, dinner parties, the Country Club."

Don't I know it, I thought. She just described August and Rose's lives. I nodded.

"I grew up in the system, Mr. Starke. Yes, I was fortunate to have Jim helping me, but my life was and is simple. I may have thought I wanted money from this family, but all I really wanted was, well, a family."

She took Jim's hand.

"If only Sandra could see you right now," Jim said.

"She can. I just know it," Mary assured him. "And she can see you, too, Jim, so put that cigar down."

He did. He extinguished it next to the first one. He soaked the tip of the cigar, and it hissed and let out a thin line of smoke that quickly dissipated.

"I didn't want the press to find out, Harry," he said. "Can you imagine the headlines? 'Judge McDowell's secret daughter' or worse. You know how the press is these days. There are some nasty types out there."

"Is that really worse than rumors of a mistress?"

Jim's eyes widened. "Who said that?"

"Just something I heard at the club," I said quickly.

Jim covered his face. "Sandra's been gone not even a week, and people are already talking." He shook his head. "Shameless."

I nodded in silent agreement, but Jim had only himself to blame. He'd put himself in the situation. People always talk; it would be stupid to expect otherwise, but it didn't mean you had to give them reasons to talk.

"That's our story, Harry. Does any of it warrant involvement of the police?" Jim asked. "I don't think so, do you?"

I thought about it. On the surface, no, there wasn't anything. It was certainly a sad story, but nothing the police would be interested in, except perhaps to eliminate the pair as suspects. Still, as Jim and Mary sat there looking at me expectantly, my gut told me there was something they weren't telling me.

I turned to Mary. "Where were you on the night Sandra died?"

"Harry!" Jim all but jumped out of his seat.

I said, "I'm sorry, but this is part of the job, Jim."

"It's okay," Mary assured both of us. "I was at home, with my daughter, sleeping. Jim called me in the morning to tell me the news, and I met him here later in the day. It was difficult."

"Of course," I said. "How about Chelsea?"

"How do you mean?" Jim asked.

"I saw her at the school, Belle Edmondson. It's none of my business, but shouldn't she be at home during these difficult times?"

"She's a strong girl, always has been," Mary said, "for as long as I've known her. We talked to her, of course, but Chels said she just couldn't sit at home and mope along with the rest of us." She said that last bit with a sad smile.

"I see. And how did she feel about this whole arrangement?" I asked, making a circular motion with my hand.

"The girls are like sisters," Jim explained. "Chelsea understands why Mary wants to stay out of the spotlight, she respects that."

Envies, maybe? I wanted to ask but didn't, and instead made a mental note to ask Chelsea a few questions next time I got the chance.

"No friction in the family, then?" I asked.

They shook their heads, and I believed them. Were they naive? Yes. Had they gotten themselves into a tricky situation? Absolutely. Had they conspired to kill Sandra McDowell? No, I didn't believe they had.

"Do you have any idea who might have killed Sandra and why?" I asked, not so much of Jim, but of Mary.

She said, "I know Jim has made a lot of enemies during his tenure on the bench but... other than that, no."

"That's an understatement," Jim said. "I've provided the police with a long list, haven't I?"

"That you have," I replied. "But no new ideas?"

"What about those killers?" Mary asked. "The Russians? The ones on the news this morning?"

I saw Jim tense, and I studied Mary for a long moment. I hadn't spoken to Kate about it yet, but apparently the news was out. I made another mental note to watch the news as soon as I got out of there to see what kind of spin they'd put on it. Russian hitmen getting shot in Chattanooga had to be a huge deal. The newscast couldn't have mentioned my part in it. If they had, Mary and McDowell would have known about it and would've said something, surely.

Did Mary know something about them? I wasn't sure. Did Jim? Maybe... I saw the tell, but I needed to be sure.

"I'm looking into that," I said, then turned to Jim. "You've seen the news also?"

"I have."

"Do you know any of those guys, Jim?" I asked, not really expecting a truthful answer.

"I've heard the names, but that was a long time ago. Aren't they retired?" Jim asked as if he wasn't aware.

"They claimed to be," I said. "But you know gangsters."

"Unfortunately, I do," Jim nodded.

"So, they had nothing to do with Sandra?" Mary asked again.

"There doesn't seem to be a connection, at least not yet. Why?"

She seemed confused for a moment but quickly recovered. "Umm, no reason. It's just that, Jim has put away a lot of bad people, including their boss—that's right, isn't it?—and I was afraid they might be coming after him next."

"Right. I agree," I said, "that's a possibility. But like I said, we don't have any proof yet. We'll know more tonight."

Okay, Harry, I thought, *now's the time. Go for it.*

"Jim," I said, looking him right in the eye. "You sentenced the Raven, Voronov, to death. How well did you get to know him?"

He quickly looked away to the left, then back again; there was something about the look: the man was about to lie to me.

"I didn't know him at all. I've always kept my distance. You know that, Harry. Why do you ask?"

I stared at him, debating with myself, *do I tell him or not? Not, I think not, for now at least.*

"No real reason," I lied. "Just thinking. Wondering why the three would be here in Chattanooga. Well, I've taken up enough of your time. I guess I'll leave you to it."

"Let me know if I can help," Jim said.

"I will," I promised, and I got up from my seat. "Er... One last question."

They both looked at me, a little guardedly, I thought.

"What do you think of Belle Edmondson?"

"The school?" Jim said, sounding surprised. "It's a fine establishment. Sandra and I have been sponsors there for, oh, twelve years or so? Ever since Chelsea first started school, we were looking for schools to support. Sandra is... was on the Belle Edmondson School Board, too."

"I know," I said. "And how did Sandra like the school?"

Jim shrugged, and Mary nodded. She said, "Sandra was always fond of the kids."

"That's not what I asked," I said sharply. "What about the staff, the faculty, the school board members?"

Jim shrugged again. "Bureaucracy, internal politics, as you'd expect, but nothing too egregious. Sandra could handle herself."

Mary grinned. "If Sandra could handle Jim McDowell, what's a couple of school officials, right?"

"That's for sure," I said, mimicking her smile, my thoughts already elsewhere. "All right, then."

Mary shook my hand, and then Jim, and I thanked them for their time and promised—again—to get to the bottom of it.

Was I getting closer? It felt like it, but at the same time, things were getting muddled. Between the shootout at the Sorbonne, Belle Edmondson, and Mary Turner—and no, I wasn't fully on board with their story—there wasn't a clear path, a chain of events for me to dissect and apply logic to.

I stood for a minute outside the house, looking up at the architecture, lost in thought. Then I shook my head, got into the Maxima, fired up the engine, and drove off, feeling... confused? That and kind of empty, if you know what I mean. I should've felt relief or satisfaction for solving the mystery of Jim's secret visitor, his de facto daughter, but I felt neither. In truth, the revelation, if it was even true, was a wrench thrown into my burgeoning theory about Sandra's death.

Perhaps Robert Rainer will shed a little light, I thought as I joined I-24 and stepped on the gas.

15

C*afe Del Luna* was a tidy little downtown organic place patronized mostly by students and office workers. I got there early for my meeting with Robert Rainer, around three-forty-five and decided to partake of a healthy meal myself.

"Menu, sir?" the waiter said, handing me a beige piece of paper. I scanned it quickly and asked for the soup of the day—split pea—and pasta carbonara. Well, perhaps, "healthy" wasn't the right word, after all.

"And coffee, please," I called after the waiter as I took out my iPhone and called Tim; he picked up on the first ring.

"Hey, Harry."

He sounded exhausted. In the background, I could hear typing and papers rustling. Tim tapped, and I was on speaker.

"Hey, Harry," Ronnie and Jacque said together. They sounded as worn-out as Tim did.

"What's up, guys? What do you have for me?" I asked.

"More than we bargained for, man," Ronnie said.

"In what way?" I said as the waiter brought my coffee.

"I didn't know what kind of school this Belle Edmondson was..." he said. "Well, I do now, but these people are serious players. Did you know the dean owns a yacht?"

Having been to the place, I wasn't exactly surprised by the revelation, but I also knew what it meant for our background checks—tons of paperwork, off-shore accounts, shell companies, and so on.

"By 'yacht' do you mean like a fishing boat?" I asked.

"I mean, yeah, you could go fishing on it. You and fifty of your buddies," Ronnie said.

"I'd go fishing on it, all right!" Jacque added. "I didn't know they sell yachts that big to common people."

"These aren't common people, Jacque," Tim said. "Far from it."

"A yacht, okay, I got it," I said. "Talk to me, guys. What else? Anything suspicious, Ronnie? Shady deals, fat account numbers? Recent transactions that seem off-kilter?"

"There's a lot still to unpack, and as much as I wanna say yes to all, I just can't, Harry. These people are squeaky-clean. They drive Bentleys and live in mansions, and that's anomalous in itself, but other than that I haven't found any criminal activity, or even anything suspicious... Not yet, but there's still a long way to go." He rustled some papers. "Lots of business deals, divorce settlements, and one woman has even patented a rubberized pencil sharpener, whatever the hell that is."

"Hold on," I said.

The waiter brought my soup and pasta, and I had to put the phone down for a moment. I reached into my jacket pocket and retrieved a pair of snow-white earbuds with a tiny microphone attached. They'd come with the iPhone. I rarely ever used them and were practically brand new. I untangled the wires, plugged the jack into my phone, and stuffed the buds into my ears.

"How's that?" I asked.

"We hear you loud and clear, Harry," Tim said.

"Good. So, there's nothing at all in the financials?"

I was grasping at straws, but I also wasn't convinced. A place that big, a private institution pulling in that much money, with so many powerful and rich people in its orbit... There had to be something. A past transgression, an altercation, some unsettled scores, embezzlement. As I've said, everyone has skeletons in their closets, so...

Ronnie said, "Nothing criminal, Harry, but I have more digging to do."

Tim said, "The Provost's son got a DUI last year, but that's about it."

I chuckled. "Is that all we can find?"

Jacque said, "Their uniforms are cute, but the skirts are too long, for my taste."

I opted not to comment on schoolgirls' skirts.

After a beat of awkward silence, I said, "Keep looking, guys. There has to be something there."

Nobody said anything, but they did let out a collective sigh. But that was their job, right? Research. I was convinced they'd find something sooner or later, even if they had to go through Belle Edmondson's entire faculty's collective biography. I admit, it bugged me, and it felt pointless trying to dig up dirt on a girls' school, but it was my best lead so far. Why? You'll think I'm crazy, but it was mostly because of what those Russian hitmen told me. Why? Well may you ask.

You see, I had nothing on them that night at the Sorbonne—before they started shooting, that is. I was just a guy talking to a bunch of old men with funny accents. Drinking at a bar, albeit a sleazy one, wasn't a crime, and there was no indication of anything more going on there. Why did they talk to me so freely? Why did they talk to me about that school? Hell, why did they talk to me at all? To ward off suspicion? Maybe.

In fact, I was willing to bet that was CPD's, and maybe even Kate's, working theory. Of course, officers were shot, so the cops would be out for blood regardless, but I had to think rationally. Those guys had no reason to lie to me.

They were definitely up to something, and they were in Chattanooga for a reason. But if they had killed Sandra, why would they hang around to celebrate? Voron's vendetta against Judge McDowell would've been fulfilled... But that's not what they said. They were there to "look after them." But what did that mean exactly? "Look after them" was mob talk for eliminating them, permanently.

Maybe that was it, and they were planning to get Jim next. But then, why get into a shootout with the police? Sure, they would've been arrested and questioned, but as those things went, professional hitmen of their pedigrees had protection. Yes, their plans would've been delayed, but nothing compared to what they'd be going up against now. Unless they were stupid, and you should never underestimate people's stupidity.

It all made little sense to me.

On the other hand, they'd given me the school which, unfortunately, was shaping up to be clean, at least so far... perhaps too clean.

Ronnie brought me out of my thoughts. "Harry, you still there?"

I set aside the empty soup bowl. "Yeah, I'm here."

It was nearing four o'clock and there was still no sign of Rainer, and I was beginning to get a bad feeling about it.

"Hey," I said, "what about Robert Rainer? Did you find anything?"

"Rings a bell," Jacque said. I heard papers being shuffled around. Then she said, "Got 'im right here. Robert Rainer, thirty-two. No criminal record. He's divorced, but has a cat named Muffins. Cute."

"So nothing odd in the guy's background?" I asked.

"Not really," she said. "Robert got a Master's in Education from the University of Tennessee in Knoxville, then came back to Chattanooga. He worked for the county for a couple of years, got a job on the staff at Belle and quickly worked his way up the ladder. Currently, he serves as the—"

"County School Board Liaison," I finished for her. "How quickly did he work his way up?" I asked for no particular reason. I doubted there was big money to be earned in college admin.

"A couple of years," Jacque said. "No untoward promotions or anything."

"Damn," I muttered and dug into the pasta. I already sensed the dead end ahead, all that was missing was the signage. "Okay, keep looking," I mumbled through a mouthful of food and almost choked doing it. I swallowed, took a drink of water, then said, "I'm supposed to be meeting Rainer in a few minutes."

"Sounds like a plan," Tim said with feigned enthusiasm. I couldn't blame him.

I clicked off, quickly finished my food, and mentally prepared myself to chat with Rainer. If his note was anything to go by, I expected him to be anxious, paranoid even. Was he just in fear of losing his job, or did he really know something? Was the school actually monitoring him, or was he headed for Moccasin Bend Mental Hospital? I reckoned I'd be finding out soon enough... but I was wrong.

At a quarter after four, I ordered another coffee and called Rainer. It went straight to voicemail. I sent him a text, and then another one ten minutes later, and followed that with another call.

Finally, I gave up and called Tim.

"Can you track Rainer's cell?" I asked and gave him the number.

I grinned at what I was doing. It was a luxury I'd never been able to enjoy before. So long as I had a phone number, Tim could find where a person was almost instantly, and even if I didn't have a number, Tim could find that too.

"Um, yeah, I guess," Tim said. "Robert Rainer? Hmm, let's see..." he said, more to himself than to me, and then typed furiously, the way only Tim could. He said, "There he is. No! Wait... the phone's inactive."

"As in turned off?"

"Either that or it's broken."

"Damn. Any way of knowing exactly how, or where the hell he is right now?" I said.

"No! I mean, yeah, sort of. I can find the location where the phone died, but not where he is right now, and that'll take time. I'd have to retrace his movements, triangulate cell towers, hack security cameras if there are any."

"Right. Let me think. Okay, get on with it. I'll call you back."

I left fifty bucks under my empty plate and left.

Geez. What the hell happened to the SOB?

16

I left *Cafe Del Luna* and drove around aimlessly, trying to think. Had I made a mistake to trust him? Was he Sandra's killer and a pathological liar who'd tricked me into leaving Belle Edmondson without asking him a single question? My face was getting hot at the mere thought of that; I wasn't usually that easily fooled. What really bothered me was that Rainer could've been long gone and out of the country.

I took a deep breath. No, he couldn't. Tim would've known. Rainer would've gotten tickets, his ID or passport would've been logged into the system, his credit cards...

Where the hell is he, then?

I stopped at the curb, took out my phone and was about to call the office, when Kate called.

"Starke," I said, all business-like, looking forward to the conversation.

"Harry, where the hell are you?" She sounded furious, and I had no idea why. My mind had already begun to run down the list of possibilities, when she said, "I need you to meet me right away."

She didn't sound happy. Bad news was acomin', I could tell.

"Of course," I said. "What's up? I just had lunch and—"

"Forget lunch, Harry. Listen. Did you go see Robert Rainer? At Belle Edmondson?"

My heart skipped a beat; I actually felt it.

"Sure," I said guardedly. "I met him there. Asked him a few questions, is all. Didn't get any answers," I said, not ready to reveal more than that before I knew what Kate's problem was.

"Must have been some hard-hitting questions, Harry, because Rainer's in the hospital. I just got the call. I'm on my way there now."

When I didn't reply, she said, "Did you hear what I said, Harry?"

"Yeah. Yeah, I did. What happened?"

"I was hoping you could tell me. Rainer's messed up pretty bad, Harry, and he's talking."

"That's good, right? Come on, Kate, out with it. The suspense is killing me."

"He claims you assaulted him," she said.

"What? You've got to be kidding me. And you believe him?"

"Of course I don't; you know I don't. But that's not relevant right now."

I must've sounded convincing because she'd calmed down... a little.

"Okay," I said. "I'm on my way to the hospital; we'll clear things up, and then I've got some questions of my own for Mr. Rainer."

"Can't promise you'll get to ask them, but yeah, I'll be waiting. CHI Memorial Hospital, Emergency Unit."

"See you in a bit."

She hung up. I sat still, thinking, growing angrier by the minute. I had nothing to worry about; I had an alibi, if my timing was right. I was at *Cafe Del Luna*. That couldn't be said for whoever had beaten up Rainer, though, and I was thoroughly pissed off.

Rainer said I assaulted him. What the hell is that about?

CHI Memorial Hospital is a huge medical complex located off Chamberlain Avenue, less than fifteen minutes from where I was parked. I made a fast U-turn and hit the gas... and then slowed quickly. I was no longer driving a police cruiser, but old habits die hard. It was just after five o'clock when I stepped out of the car that afternoon.

The day had been nice and warm, but just as I pulled into the visitors' parking lot, it began to rain. I'd dated a girl back in high school, who was going to study cinema, and she'd told me that rain in the movies hinted that something bad or sad was about to happen. I'd scoffed at the idea then, but at that moment I found myself looking up at the heavy, overcast sky with something akin to trepidation.

"There you are, thank God," Kate said when I stepped through the main entrance doors.

I smiled when I saw her, but then I saw Henry Finkle standing behind her, and suddenly I knew my high school date had been right. My mood plunged deep into the black.

What the hell is he doing here?

"Starke!" the man barked. "You have some nerve—"

"Cool it, Henry," I snarled at him. "Who kicked your frickin' cat? What the hell's going on?"

"Oh, like you don't know," Finkle said. "I knew it was only a matter of time before you crossed the line. I'm glad I'm here to witness it. I might just put the cuffs on you myself."

"Bravo, Henry. You wish, you sneaky little shit," I said.
"Try it and I'll bust your ass."

"You're really pushing it, Starke," he snarled.

"Yeah, I am. Bite me," I said and I turned to Kate. "So, what's up?"

But Assistant Chief Finkle wasn't done, "Listen here, Starke—"

"Henry," Kate said, interrupting him, "take it easy, okay? Harry showed up, didn't he? Now let's get to the bottom of this mess. Come on, let's go see Rainer."

She waved for me to follow her, and I did, walking past the still fuming Henry Finkle. Whatever he thought I'd done, he wouldn't get the satisfaction of seeing me squirm under some vague threat he'd never be able to fulfill.

A nurse took us down the long hallway to Robert Rainer's room, which was guarded by not one but two uniformed officers, neither of whom was thrilled to see me. Tough shit.

"Harry," Kate said, "I need you to surrender your weapon, please."

I raised an eyebrow but did as I was asked. There was no reason to make a scene over it.

"Nice and slowly, Starke," Finkle said.

I gave him a sharp look as I took out my Smith & Wesson and handed it to one of the frowning officers.

"Be careful with that," I said. "It's loaded, and there's one in the chamber. Don't shoot yourself, or anyone else... and I'll need it back."

"We'll see about that," Finkle said.

I just shook my head.

Kate stepped into the room first, then me, then Finkle close behind, too close for comfort. What did he think I was going to do? Attack Rainer in his hospital bed in front of four cops?

Rainer's eyes widened when he saw me, and I know damn well he would have been up out of the bed and away had both his arms and right leg not been in casts.

"What the hell is he doing here?" Rainer asked, staring at me.

"You have nothing to worry about, Mr. Rainer," Finkle said. "Sergeant Gazzara and myself will make sure this man doesn't touch you... again."

"For God's sake, Henry, get off my back," I said. "I haven't touched him, nor am I planning to do so. You, on the other hand, I might just make an exception—"

"Are you threatening me, Starke?" he said, interrupting me.

"We'll never know now, will we?" I said. "You didn't let me finish."

"Boys, please," Kate said. "You're both big and scary... Well, you're big, Harry."

I had to smile at that one.

She turned to the man in the bed. "Now please, Mr. Rainer, tell us again exactly what happened."

He swallowed hard and said, "Him, it was him, Harry Starke. He came by the school earlier today, asking questions. Then, when I went to lunch, at a burger place across the road, he caught up with me, asking all these questions... He roughed me up pretty bad."

"This is bullshit, Kate," I said, quietly, my arms folded across my chest.

I studied Rainer's face, trying to understand what game he was playing and why.

"You did," Rainer said. "I didn't answer your questions, so you started kicking me."

"Not true," I said.

"But is it true, Starke?" Finkle asked.

"Are you shitting me, Henry?" I asked, astounded that he would even think I was capable of... Okay, let's not go there.

"Come on," I said. "We don't have to like each other, but I know you're not *that* stupid. And you know I'm not stupid enough to show up at the bedside of the guy I'd supposedly assaulted, and with four cops present."

"Maybe you are, maybe you aren't," Finkle said in a weak voice.

Kate said, "Mr. Rainer, could you explain the nature of Mr. Starke's questions?"

"He asked me about Sandra McDowell. What her job was and if she had any enemies who might've wished her dead."

He looked away. He seemed to be both sad and... embarrassed? But by what exactly? I thought I knew— Robert was lying through his teeth because he had to, and he was a terrible liar.

"Who did this to you, Robert?" I asked. "Really?"

He didn't reply. He just shook his head, wouldn't make eye contact.

Was it someone from the school? I wondered. Had they bugged his hospital room, too? It sounded absurd, crazy even, but stranger things have happened.

Kate said, "Mr. Rainer, I can promise you that we'll keep you safe. There are two officers outside your door. Their orders are to stay there at all times until we find who did this to you. But we really need your help... Look, we all know it wasn't Harry, and we all know that you know who it really was. So please tell us and let's get them off the street."

He looked up at her, even managed a small smile, but then he just shook his head and said nothing.

And then Kate's phone pinged; she had a text message.

As she took it out of her pocket, Henry's phone buzzed too. They both looked at their screens. They looked at each other, obviously stunned, both of them.

"What the—" Finkle said.

"Holy cow," Kate said.

Then my iPhone buzzed. The message was from Ronnie:

Voron has escaped! He's in the wind!

17

We stood there, the three of us, frozen to the spot, for a long moment, staring at our phones like complete morons, then at each other.

"What is it?" Rainer asked, his eyes shifting between us.

"Probably nothing," Henry Finkle replied. "Not our concern."

"Very much our concern," Kate said. "Come on, we need to go."

I didn't move, so Henry looked me straight in the eye and said, "You're going, too, Starke."

"No, I'm not," I said. "Unless you're arresting me for assaulting Robert Rainer, which I'm pretty sure we've discovered never happened."

I glanced at Rainer, and so did Henry.

Rainer shook his head, said nothing.

Henry grunted, and Kate started toward the door.

"Let's go, we've got work to do," she said.

"And so do I," I said.

The two of them left the room, Henry saying, "I don't

see what this has to do with us," as he went through the doors.

One of the uniformed officers squinted at me as he shut the door but didn't say anything. Rainer was silent this whole time, staring at me, patiently waiting.

"So?" he said, "are going to tell me what's going on?"

"There's no need," I said, taking a seat next to Rainer's cot. "It's police business. You'll see it on the news any time now." I saw his panicked face and added, "It has nothing to do with you, Robert."

I wasn't sure that was entirely true... at least, I couldn't be one hundred percent sure, not then anyway.

"Okay, Robert," I said gently. "Who did this to you?"

His shoulders twitched, which I took for a shrug. Evidently, the man was still in a lot of pain.

"I don't know," he said.

"Work with me here, Robert. Whoever did this was sending a message, so who could the message be from?"

He only shook his head, obviously scared stupid.

"Listen," I said. "It's okay to be scared, but nothing's going to happen to you, I promise. There are two officers outside this door, and I know CPD can and will keep you safe. Sergeant Gazzara will see to that."

She will if I can convince her to treat him as a witness, an important one. And all the little SOB needs to do is give me something to work with.

I waited, watching him. He couldn't hold eye contact with me, then he twitched again, shook his head.

"I don't know them, Mr. Starke."

"Them. That's good, Robert, really good. Call me Harry, okay? How many were there?"

"Two men. Maybe about my age, maybe a little older, but not much. I'd never seen them before."

"A little older?" I said.

Damn!

I was hoping to hear him describe the two Russian hitmen. It would've made little sense if it had been them, but then again, nothing did... make sense.

"They had buzz cuts and wore black windbreakers. I saw sports shoes when they kicked me."

He closed his eyes at the memory, or maybe the pain, but he didn't cry. I waited.

"Why would they hurt me?" he whispered.

There was something cartoony about it. He reminded me of a child trying to trick his parents. But what was his trick?

"That's what I'm going to find out, Robert. You can take that to the bank."

I paused, thought for a moment, then said, "I don't get it, Robert. They didn't say anything? That makes no sense. They didn't warn you... maybe tell you to keep your mouth shut, stay away from me?"

He shook his head, looked miserable.

I produced the note he'd passed to me when we first met and held it up.

"About this," I said. "Why?"

"Oh, that. I didn't want anyone at the office to hear us."

"How do you mean? Is someone monitoring the offices?"

"That's what I've heard. Sounds stupid..." He shook his head as if disappointed with himself.

"Nothing stupid about it," I said. "Anything you can tell me helps, Robert."

"Ugh. It's a rumor the girls have been sharing for years. The students, I mean. They say the school is run by some evil corporation that has eyes and ears on everyone. It's silly, one of those conspiracy theories, you know?"

I nodded, understanding. Every school has one of those stories. In my first year at McCallie, someone spread a rumor that our... well, no point in churning up that old mud. We never learned who started the rumor, but let's just say that kids can be cruel.

But what Rainer was telling me sounded like... well, something more. A school-wide conspiracy: bugged admin offices, a member of the staff—Rainer—beaten half to death... and Sandra's death. Was there a grander scheme afoot, or was I simply grasping at straws?

"So, what's the theory?" I asked. "Who's listening?"

Rainer shrugged. "The evil president of the school?" he actually smiled, though I could tell that it hurt him to do so. "The Illuminati? Your guess is as good as mine. When you came in this morning, I panicked, Mr. Starke. Thought it would be better if we talked elsewhere."

"You weren't wrong."

"Look where it got me."

I looked at him. *Whoever it was, sure as hell did a number on him.*

Rainer would be out of commission for months. *I hope he has good insurance, poor bastard.*

"So there's really no conspiracy?" I asked. "No evil faculty?"

He tilted his head, winced, then said, "Of course not. At least, not that I know of, Mr. Starke... Do you mind if I rest for a while now? I need some sleep."

"Yes, of course. Thank you for your time, Robert."

He closed his eyes, and I got up to leave. I was about to close the door when I turned my head to glance at him. He was watching me through half-closed eyes. He closed them as soon as he saw me look at him.

Something's not right here, I thought. *Robert Rainer, you're full of it.*

I grabbed my pistol from the cop outside the door, holstered it, then took off down the corridor toward the exit.

18

I called Kate as soon as I stepped outside the hospital.

"It's a bit busy here, Harry," she said instead of a greeting.

"What's the word out there?" I asked.

"Voron is on the run, in Nashville."

"How the hell did they manage to pull it off?" I asked.

"Money, Harry, lots of money, *big* money. They're still trying to figure it out, but apparently, the riot was staged by a cadre of heavily bribed prisoners. They kept the riot going and escalating. In addition, several of the death row guards were also bribed; two for sure, but possibly three. They waited for the riot to peak, then they disabled the two remaining guards, got Voron out of his cell, dressed him in a guard's uniform and cap, covered his face and shirt with blood, and hauled him out to a waiting ambulance.

"The ambulance was stopped and searched at the main gate on the way out, but the guards there saw only a badly wounded and unconscious guard—apparently leaking copious quantities of blood—two EMTs and the driver, and they let them through."

"Dammit. Any dead?" I asked.

"Surprisingly, no... which is amazing, considering what Voron is. But it seems the rioters went out of their way to injure as many guards as possible, but not to kill. There were eleven at the last count, most of them with broken bones."

"That must have been intentional," I said. "To cause as much mayhem and damage as possible to draw attention away from the real target, Voron."

"So it would seem," she said thoughtfully. "Whatever, it worked. He got away."

"How about Tesak and Brick?" I said, already figuring out the timeline in my head. "Any signs of them being involved? We know they must have been."

"It's possible they were in Nashville. There's a BOLO out for them, there and here, but so far, nothing."

"Anything on the prison CCTV security system?"

"I'd say there is, has to be, but Nashville isn't talking to us. They're trying to keep it in-house, but you know how that goes, right?"

"Oh yeah, only too well. I'd say some folks at Riverbend are in deep doo-doo. You'll keep me updated, right?"

"I'll let you know if something comes up. Gotta go Harry. Talk to you later."

"Thanks, Kate," I said, but she'd already clicked off.

I jumped into the Maxima and headed west on East 3rd toward my office.

So, the two hitmen were in Nashville, I thought, *which means they couldn't have attacked Rainer... Or were they? Sheesh... Who bribed the guards and organized the escape team if they didn't? That would have taken a lot of planning and, as Kate said, a whole lot of cash... Well, Voron has that! So... it must have been Tesak... Yeah, Tesak, because someone had to plan the op, coordinate the prison riot, pay off the guards, and organize the med team. Geez... Yeah, Tesak. Brick doesn't have the brains.*

I turned left on Lindsey, right on East 4th, then left onto Georgia Avenue, my mind churning all the way.

But... if the two of them were out of town, that would mean Rainer was attacked by someone else, and for some other reason. Something tells me his story stinks. Buzz cut? Who the hell has one of those these days; they went out in the sixties. I think he knows exactly who attacked him and why. He was frickin' playing me, the little shit.

I almost turned the car and went back to confront the sneaky bastard, but I didn't, and afterward wished I had. Anyway, three minutes later I was parked in the lot outside my office and heading for the side door.

I opened the door and stepped inside to hear Jacque's Jamaican accent even before the door closed behind me.

"Harry, what a surprise! Come on in!" She was in the front office standing behind her desk. "I have the front door locked. We're all in the conference room."

"You have the door locked?" I asked, eyebrows raised. "What if a client wants in?"

"He or she will be the first, that's for sure. Anyway, Tim put one of those new-fangled, fancy video doorbells out there. We'll know."

I shook my head. "Jacque, you just destroyed a dream. I was hoping that one day I'd be in my office and you'd show in some beautiful 'dame' with an unsolvable problem. You'd be Velda to my Mike Hammer."

"I'd be what to whom?" she said, a puzzled frown on her face.

She obviously had no idea what I was talking about, but then neither did any of them, especially Tim.

"Never mind," I said, with a sigh. "I'll get some coffee and join you in the conference room."

"You will not," she said. "I'll get it. You go sit down. By the look on your face, you need more than just coffee... You want me to add a little somethin' to it?"

Oh boy, was I ever tempted? I was, and I'm not going to lie to you...

"Why not, Jacque?" I said. "Just a splash of Laphroaig, and I do mean just a splash."

"Sure you do, boss," she said, hurrying away.

"Stop calling me that," I yelled after her.

I walked into the conference room with a huge smile on my face. Tim was on the floor with his laptop on his knees, his back to the wall. Ronnie was at the table, surrounded by paperwork.

"Working hard, I see?" I said.

Ronnie looked up to me with red eyes. "You know, Harry, if you'd told me this would be part of my job—"

"For which you're handsomely compensated, yes," I interrupted him. "Please continue," I said, grinning widely, as I sat down next to him.

"Well, you got me there, man." Ronnie smirked. "Hey, you're in a good mood. What's up?"

"I am. I really am. So. Did you find anything?"

Jacque handed me a huge mug of black coffee filled to the brim. I took a sip and almost choked: not from the heat of the liquid, but from the "splash" she'd added to it.

I looked at her, my lips pursed. She grinned at me and sat down.

"Enjoy!" she said.

I shook my head, and said, "Ronnie?"

"More of the same," he said. "Old money, new money,

but nothing criminal. These guys are as clean as they come."

"Right, so let's take a break from it, and thanks guys, good job on this."

Tim looked up. "Really?"

"Of course. Even you are human... I think. Unless there's a mother ship waiting for you somewhere. Can't win 'em all." I thought for a minute then shook my head and said, "I still think something's off about that school, but I'll have to find another way to find out what that is." I got up and paced around the table. "There must be something I'm missing..."

"Any news on Voron?" Ronnie asked.

"No, not yet, but I have one of those feelings... Half of the state's police forces are on his ass, searching for him. Kate said he had accomplices, at least eight, not including our two Russian friends, Tesak and Brick. I don't think we've heard the last—"

"Holy shit, Harry," Jacque said, interrupting me. "You sure it's safe for you out there?"

That was the first time I'd ever heard her curse. Jacque was, is... there's no other word for it, she's awesome. The gods were definitely smiling down on me that day when I walked into my doctor's office and found her there. She's one of the most caring people I know. Back then, when we first started the agency, she was still very nervous about the kind of work I did and the methods I used. She was very protective of me, and she could be a little overbearing at times, but this time... I had the strongest feeling she might be right.

"I'm not sure," I said. "I doubt they broke Voron out to come after me. Revenge for Paper Boy, maybe, but I hardly think so."

"Would *they* agree with that?" Ronnie said. "Let's face it, Harry. It would be easy enough to terminate you."

He paused, shook his head, closed his eyes, and then continued, "This is freakin' ridiculous. We're in this thing like we're bit players in some 1940s B movie."

I laughed. "I was just talking to Velda... Jacque, about that very thing. Okay, let's be serious for a minute. Tesak and Brick might come after me, though I wouldn't recommend it, but they wouldn't need Voron for that," I reasoned out loud. "Hell, anyone can find me at any time."

They all remained silent as I paced the room, thinking: Tim tapped on his computer, then looked up at me and said, "What about that guy Rainer?"

"Oh, yeah. Someone's put him in the hospital; he'll be there for a while. They did a hell of a number on him."

"Someone?" Tim asked.

"Wasn't me, if that's what you're implying," I said, but I grinned at him.

"Who then?"

"Some guys, so he says. Buzz cuts and windbreakers, big guys, aged around thirty. Sound like anyone you know, Ronnie?"

He bellowed a laugh. "Sounds like most people I know, well, except for the buzz cuts. People, sane people, don't have their hair cut like that anymore."

"That's why I asked," I said and looked at my watch. "It's almost seven. You guys go home, get some rest. I'll see you back here tomorrow morning. I'm going to go visit Benny Hinkle, see if he can shed a little light."

"You sure that's wise, man?" Ronnie said, his face creased with concern. "His place just got shot up. The police are all over his ass. You think he'll talk to you?"

"I have ways of making him talk, Ronnie, as you well

know. Do like I told you. Go home, get some rest." I turned and headed for the door. "Sheesh, I could use some rest myself," I mumbled, more to myself than to them, as I walked.

Lookout, Benny! Here I come.

19

The last couple of days had been hectic. I don't think I'd ever had an investigation this confounding in all of my career with the PD. One thing I was glad about was my new status as a private investigator. There were a lot of perks to it, being my own boss was just one of them. Beyond that, though, I was free from the constraints of officialdom: office politics, protocols, reports, warrants, and subpoenas were all necessary investigatory tools, but they could also slow down or even kill an investigation. I, on the other hand, now had the freedom to move around and talk to people as I pleased, and I was accountable to no one, other than myself and my clients.

Benny Hinkle had most certainly talked to the cops, but they always gave him a little slack, so there was no telling how reliable his info was. But like I told Ronnie, I had ways of making Benny talk, tell me things he would never tell another soul. I'm talking about another perk of being an independent agent—bribery and, if necessary, physical violence. Oh yeah, that too.

See, Benny Hinkle was like a slot machine. You fed him

cash, and most of the time you'd hit a couple of cherries, hear things you already knew. However, sometimes he could be persuaded to spit out a jackpot, and that was what I needed.

I had a bunch of threads, developments, and suspicions, none of which made any sense. Assassins, supposedly retired; a prestigious school where things might be what they seem; two mystery assailants; Jim McDowell himself and his... whatever, daughter; Voron, the Raven, that had to be connected, though for the life of me I couldn't see how; Robert Rainer, the lying little sack of... and the list goes on... I was hoping Benny could give me something to connect the threads.

I drove past the front entrance to the Sorbonne. It was still taped off, and there was a shabby "CLOSED" sign on the door. I took a right turn onto Prospect and parked at the curb. The bloodstain on the pavement where officer Florez was shot was still visible, but otherwise, the street was clean.

The rear exit door, the one I'd charged out of, wasn't locked. I opened it and stepped through into the darkened passageway.

"Hello, Benny. You there?"

"Who's there?" he yelled.

As I neared the main bar room, I heard someone sweeping. It was brightly lit, and empty—both scenarios I'd never seen before—and so quiet; the raspy old speakers were silent. And then I saw her.

Who the...

"Laura?" I said. "Look at you. I barely recognized you."

Benny's trusty number two was in the middle of the room, sweeping glass shards and wood chips into a long-handled dustpan on the floor. Laura was wearing jeans and an uncharacteristically long-sleeved shirt with a black V-neck top underneath that gave no hint at a cleavage. Her hair was tied back in a ponytail.

"Hey, Harry," she said. "Tell me you're here for a shift change."

"Afraid not," I said. "Didn't they send in cleaners?"

It was standard procedure to send professional cleaners to a crime scene to get rid of the aftermath of a shooting, but evidently, they figured a few bloodstains weren't worth it.

"They did," Laura said, "but they didn't do shit. So, Mr. Hinkle over there," she pronounced Benny's last name with sarcasm, "called me in to do their job."

The Southern accent was soft, real, not the caricature she affected when on duty, and it brought joy to my heart, even though the rest of the picture was beyond depressing.

"I'm sorry to hear that," I said, as I walked past her.

I stood and stared at the blood that stained the booth the three Russians had occupied. The floor was littered with wood-splinters. Bullet holes in the table, seats and the wall behind the booth were marked with small color-coded pieces of tape and told a story all their own. It appeared that three officers had returned fire in that direction... maybe two dozen shots in all.

Laura said, "What the hell did you say to those assholes that they started shooting, Harry?"

"Me? Nothing," I said.

I wanted to say more, but Benny Hinkle stepped out from behind the bar. He had a drink in his hand, and by the look on his face, he wasn't pleased to see me; not one bit.

"What do *you* want, Starke?"

It never ceased to amaze me how much he looked like Danny DeVito. He was wearing a black T-shirt, huge khaki shorts that came all the way down to mid-calf, and leather sandals.

"The same thing I always want from you, Benny. A drink, a few words, and some information." I went to the bar and climbed up onto a stool.

Benny stared at me, obviously considered his options, then he turned around and walked back behind the bar.

I heard a disgusted grunt, turned around, and saw Laura shaking her head. I grinned at her. She stuck her tongue out at me and then continued sweeping.

"I'll have a beer," I said.

Benny's selection of whiskey would've put me in the hospital, and no I didn't expect him to pour me a shot of the good stuff that Laura usually did when her boss wasn't looking.

He passed me a cold bottle of Corona from the lit-up mini-fridge. It wasn't my preference, but it was better than nothing, and it was cold.

"I've already talked to the cops, Harry."

"I'm sure you have, Benny. But I was here that night, so I know what went down." I didn't, not exactly, but he didn't have to know that. "That's not what I wanted to talk to you about."

"What, then?"

I sighed. "Let's make it quick and easy, Benny, all right?"

I had little patience for Benny's antics that night, but I was too tired to go through the ritual, so I unholstered the S&W and laid it on the counter in front of me, then I reached for my wallet. The first bill I came up with was a fifty and laid it beside the gun.

"What's it to be, Benny?"

"What do you think, Starke," he said as he reached out and took the money. "What do you wanna know?"

"Two guys, big, early thirties, buzz cuts, windbreakers. Sound familiar?"

"Well, yeah, a lot of people. You'll have to be more specific."

I shook my head. "I can't. That's it."

"I can't help you. The description is too vague... *buzz cuts?* Who does that anymore? What else ya got?"

I figured it was a long shot, but... "Have you heard about Vlad Voronov?"

"The Russian hitman who escaped Riverbend today? Sure," Benny said, taking a swig of his drink. "What of it?"

"The guys who shot up his place," I said. "They're his friends. The cops think they helped him escape, and I tend to agree."

"Really, Harry? What a coincidence," he said sarcastically, not the least bit impressed.

"Let me help you connect the dots, Benny. Think for a minute: suppose the word got out on the street that the owner of the Sorbonne had snitched on them to the cops and, consequently, one of them was killed. Where would you be then, huh?"

He looked at me, uncomfortable, and said, "You wouldn't."

"Wouldn't I? That doesn't have to happen, Benny, but I need to know where they're hiding."

He held my gaze, raised his eyebrows, so I passed him another banknote.

He said, "I might know a guy who knows a guy who might be able to tell you."

20

"Spill it, Benny. I don't have time for games."
"D'you wanna hear the intel or not?" Benny
asked, taking another sip of his crappy whiskey.

*Geez, give him half an inch and he'll steal a frickin'
yard.*

I placed another fifty on the table but yanked it back
when he reached for it.

"Not so fast," I said. "Talk."

"I told ya, I heard something from a guy who heard it
from a guy—"

"Not the best beginning, Benny," I said, and I sipped
my beer.

"It's what I got," he replied. "People talk, I listen. You
know how it goes. So, there's this guy, Tony Paolo, right?"

Oh yes, I know Tony.

"A friend of his," he continued, "keeps a... um, a shel-
ter... Yeah, let's call it that. Well, that friend told Tony
there were a couple of Russians in there yesterday, catching their
breath. Said they were the guys who shot up my bar."

"And you heard this from Tony the Sharpie?" I asked.

Tony "The Sharpie" Paolo was a small-time crook, who dabbled in drugs and guns, but mostly stuck to white-collar crime—book cooking, fake IDs, that sort of thing. The word on the street was that Tony had earned his nickname back in first grade, when he used a Sharpie marker to write a note from his parents explaining that little Tony was too sick to go to school. Sharpie's methods had improved since then, but the name stuck.

"He doesn't like to be called that, Harry," Benny said.

"I don't give a rat's ass what Sharpie likes, and I'm gonna need more than his word. For all I know, he saw it on the news."

Benny shrugged. "Who hasn't? Except, Sharpie says they've stayed there before that."

"My people tell me they stayed at a motel," I said.

"Hah, some hot-shot PI you are," he said and grinned. "What'd they do, your people, track their cell phones? You think those old guys are stupid, or what? They know better'n you and 'your people' how everything works, how to stay under the radar. The bastards have been hiding from you, Starke."

I studied his face, looking for signs of a lie; he was an easy read. But he was collected, not the least bit bothered. He downed what was left of the glass of whiskey in a single gulp. Obviously, he was comfortable... Why wouldn't he be? He was simply selling information.

I took my hand off the bill, and he grabbed it and stuffed it into a pocket of his shorts.

"Pleasure doing business with you, Starke."

"I bet, but we're not done yet. Where's the hideout?"

He shook his head. "Even if I knew, do you think I'd tell ya? What would the boys say if they found out I give up safe houses? Not a good look, huh?" He poured himself more whiskey.

He turned again to face me. I picked up the S&W, leaned across the bar, grabbed him by the neck of his T-shirt and pulled him toward me. Whiskey slopped all over the bar, and me.

I was just about to tap the bridge of his nose with the barrel of the gun when I happened to look into his eyes; he was petrified with fear and... for some weird reason even I couldn't figure, I believed him, and I let him go.

"Geez, Harry," he gasped. "There's no need for that. You know I'd tell ya if I knew, I don't know where it is. I don't."

"I believe you, Benny. You haven't got the balls to lie to me. Tell me about Sharpie. I haven't heard from him in a while," I said. "Does he still work at Finley Stadium?"

"Last I heard, yeah," Benny said, "Tony was promoted to head of security there, doing well for himself. Got a house, nice new car an' all."

"I'm happy for him." I finished the beer and set the bottle down. "Put it on my tab, Benny."

"Funny, Starke."

I slid off the stool and headed toward the emergency exit.

"Good luck, you two," I said to Laura, who only scoffed.

I glanced at my watch as I got into the car. It was just after eight o'clock, and probably too late to catch Sharpie at work, which would've been best. I wanted him to be uncomfortable, nervous, preferably among other people who weren't aware of his main source of income.

21

Half an hour later I was back in my condo, barely standing after another exhausting day. It was dark outside, no moon, no stars, just a blanket of heavy gray clouds drifting slowly over the city. The surface of the river was like glass, the reflections of the lights on the Thatcher Bridge stilettoes of liquid gold. I poured myself a drink and called Kate.

"Hey, Harry," she said, her voice sounded as tired as I felt.

"Hey, Kate. Long day?"

"Keeps getting longer, too. Robert Rainer is in a coma. Apparently, he was hit on the head, too, and that hit caused a delayed reaction in his brain, like an echo of a concussion."

"Jesus... Poor guy. Somebody was trying to scare him to death, literally."

"Not funny, Harry," she said.

"I know; it wasn't meant to be. It's just... this whole thing is a mess. Have you talked to Jim McDowell?"

"Not since the initial interview, why? Did he tell you something?"

"He did," I said. "But I'm not sure how it figures into the picture yet."

"Care to share with the class, Harry?"

The truth was, I didn't know how telling Kate about Mary would affect my investigation. On the surface of things, Mary's existence in itself had no correlation to any of our suspects. She was, in effect, Jim McDowell's adoptive daughter, in fact if not on paper, and that was all there was to it... or was it? I had one of those feelings that there was more to Mary Turner than either she or Jim let on.

"Harry?" she said.

"Yes! I'm here. Okay, so..." and I told her everything I knew.

"Holy cow," was Kate's conclusion.

"Well, I wouldn't go that far. I asked Tim to look into her background, and he found nothing untoward... and if Tim didn't find anything, there's nothing to be found."

"That's not the point, Harry. If Judge McDowell kept the existence of a daughter from you, who knows what other secrets he's keeping?"

"None that I nor Tim, nor Ronnie for that matter, could dig up, Kate. He's clean... squeaky clean. My read is that Jim's a new widower and doesn't know how to live with it yet. But maybe you should talk to him, but go easy on him, okay? He's hurting."

"Maybe I will," she said.

"Anything on Voron and his pals?" I asked.

"Nope. The trail's cold. He's disappeared, like a freakin' phantom. No leads, nothing. We're not even sure they're still in the state. The feds have put them on their most wanted list, put out APBs, the whole nine yards. The Canadian border is on high alert, so are all the major airports. It's all covered." She sounded more and more exhausted as she went down the list.

"Sounds huge. Are we about to have an international scandal on our hands?" I asked. "The last thing I need is for my investigation to turn into a publicity crapshoot."

"The Russians claim they're in no way affiliated with Voron, Harry, as you'd expect, and they don't seem at all bothered by any of it. To them, Voron is just another escaped convict."

I thought for a minute, but could come up with little else worth saying, so I didn't.

"See you tonight?" I said.

"Doubt it. There's too much to do still."

"We should go on a date tomorrow," I said. "A nice place, red wine, dessert menus—"

"We'll see," she said and hung up.

I thought for a minute; there was something I needed to do so, tired as I was, I decided to go out again. Have dinner at the Public House—a nice steak with a baked potato—and then I went to Chestnut Street and spent the best part of an hour studying Finley Stadium, the home of the CFC—the Chattanooga Football Club, only it wasn't football they played, it was soccer.

I called Ronnie from my car and asked him to do a little digging into Tony "The Sharpie" Paolo—yes, I said Ronnie. I didn't want to bother Tim this late at night, even though I had a feeling he was probably lost in some online game, so I asked Ronnie to make some calls instead, and he didn't disappoint.

An hour later I was back home and we were on the phone, and he was briefing me on Sharpie's biography.

There wasn't much to it. The word on the street was

that Sharpie was indeed sharp, knew what he was doing, which is why the CPD couldn't touch him. On paper, Tony Paolo was legit. Head of security at the stadium, with sixteen people under his supervision and a broad network of ancillaries from private security to chauffeurs to catering. He lived with his girlfriend Tami in a nice suburban house and drove a brand-new BMW X3.

"Thanks, Ronnie," I said and hung up.

It wasn't much, but I now had a half-assed plan of action in my head, so I took a quick shower and went to bed.

22

Next morning, I had to catch up with some routine chores—I still wasn't used to the corporate workaday world and quickly found myself running out of time. I wanted to catch Tony Paolo unawares and was running late. Anyway, as I was on my way to Finley Stadium, I got a call from Tim.

"Hey, Tim. What's up?" I said. "Have you found something for me?"

"I'm pretty sure I have. It's about Mary Turner."

"Let me guess, Jim McDowell bankrolled her education? I know."

Tim was silent for a moment, and then he said, "Well, yeah, she's basically his daughter, but that's not all. I went all the way back to her childhood, to check out her parents. You know, maybe they wanted to reconnect with Mary and couldn't handle her new rich family."

"Yes, and?"

"Well I didn't find anything," Tim said.

"How do you mean?"

"The files are incomplete, but the records list her parents as unknown."

"That's not unusual, Tim, unfortunately. Plenty of kids grow up not knowing who their folks are," I said.

"I know, I know, but the odd thing is... How do I explain it? Okay, so, sometimes guys like me... well, we hack stuff for fun, right?"

"I won't ask you to clarify that, but go on," I replied, intrigued.

"When we hack into places, we sometimes... well, we leave little marks—tags—in the code, to let other hackers know we've been there."

"Like a serial killer's signature?" I asked, my mind wandering into the scary places.

"More like a graffiti tag, but yes."

"And you found a tag... where?"

"Several tags in several databases, all of them with Mary Turner's name thereon."

I was quiet for a minute, letting the information sink in.

"Could it be a coincidence?" I asked. "I'm sure you're not the only one peeking into those databases through unofficial channels."

"Could be," Tim said. "Except, this tag appears only in Mary Turner's files."

"Which means what?"

"It means, Harry, that Mary Turner is a plant."

"You're kidding, right?" I asked, knowing darned well that he wasn't.

"I'll do you one better, Harry. I know who planted her there."

I could just imagine Tim beaming as he said it.

"What would I do without you, Tim?" I asked. "Nice

job, but look, I have to go. Right now, I'm on a mission. We'll talk later. I'll be in the office early this afternoon, and we'll look into it then."

"Sounds like a plan."

I hung up. *Damn it, Jim.* Why the hell wouldn't he tell me? And what did this even mean? Could Mary Turner actually be Mary McDowell, Jim's illegitimate daughter? What other reason could there be for him to falsify her identity?

All that would have to be dealt with later; I turned into the mostly empty parking lot of the stadium and killed the engine.

Finley Stadium was, is a relatively large arena that could sit just over twenty thousand people. I used to come here a lot during high school to watch soccer and yes, football too. There was no game that day, so I walked straight on up to the box office, where a lonely clerk was browsing Facebook on her work computer.

"Excuse me?" I said.

"Oh, hey," she said. "How can I help?"

"My name's Harry Starke. I'm here to see... Anthony Paolo."

"Tony? He's in the office. What's this about?" she said frowning.

"I'm conducting an investigation into Sandra McDowell's death," I said as seriously as I could.

"That judge's wife? Oh, that's horrible, am I right? What's Tony got to do with it?"

"I'm not at liberty to discuss it, ma'am. Could you point me to Tony's office, please?"

She did, and I smiled at the thought that if Sharpie was in charge of security, he wasn't so good at his job. The clerk just let in a stranger without even asking for his ID.

Sharpie's office was down a narrow corridor beyond the stadium entrance, past the restrooms and staff rooms. I knocked on the door.

"Come in."

I did.

The office was surprisingly spacious—it contained a guest couch, a cupboard, an L-shaped desk with two computer monitors on it, two guest chairs, and a large leather chair occupied by Sharpie himself. Two guys in their early forties were seated in the guest chairs.

Uh-oh! I thought.

Tony Paolo was a thin man, close to fifty, with lively eyes and a balding head. He wore a white golf shirt and tan pants. His "Security" windbreaker hung on a hook on the wall behind him. He stopped smiling when he saw me. I knew all about him, but we'd never met, not even back when I was a cop, but he must've smelled it on me.

"Who are you?" he asked.

"Harry Starke, private investigator."

Tony's guests exchanged looks. He told them, "Could you guys step outside for a few minutes?"

They did, stepping around me and exiting the way I'd come in. I noticed there was another door behind Tony, too.

"Please, take a seat," he said with a professional smile.

I did. "Those guys security?" I asked.

"Interviewees," Tony explained. "We're expanding our staff for the next season."

"Are you, now? Have I missed the news of the Super-bowl coming to Chattanooga?"

"You mock, but I care about safety around here."

"That's what I hear, Sharpie," I said, looking him in the eye.

He frowned, and his nose twitched slightly. I figured he wasn't the best poker player.

As his face began to turn red, Tony Paolo cleared his throat and said, "What do you want?"

"Safety, as you said."

"I don't follow," Tony said, leaning back in his chair.

"What do you know about a group of Russian contract killers? There were three of them."

"Oh, yeah, I saw the news. That's messed up. Did you catch them?" he asked.

I decided to play along. "Not yet, no. I was hoping you could help me, Tony."

"Me? How would I be able to help?"

"Why do they call you Sharpie?" I asked in turn.

"Nobody calls me that," he growled.

"Sure they do. Something to do with fake IDs, isn't that right?"

"I don't follow."

"Okay, we've screwed around long enough. Let's cut to the reason I'm here. Sharpie, I know you keep a safe house for lowlifes that need a place to lay low from the cops. I also know you hosted the Russians while they planned a prison break, and after a shootout that put a cop in the hospital. So talk to me, before I feel the need to... well, you get the idea, don't you, Sharpie?"

He nodded, slowly, considering my words, and then he said, "You know, the last time I saw them, one of them said I might get a visit from some obnoxious private dick. They weren't kidding. You're one nosy piece o' shit, you know that? You come into my office, thinking you can pressure me into giving them up. Well, screw you, Starke."

My body tensed. I'd expected him to give me something, but he was giving more than I'd asked for.

"Boys!" he called.

The two guys were in the room in a second. I turned to look at them. They were huge. I'm six-two, but these guys were both pushing six-five, and they were built like bulls: probably ex-football players earning a living as Sharpie's muscle.

"Do you know your boss is a criminal, guys?" I asked.

They exchanged another look and laughed heartily. I turned back to Sharpie.

I said, "I wouldn't do anything stupid, Sharpie. I'm not alone, and you just confessed to aiding and abetting."

Sharpie grinned. "I did, didn't I? You think I'm stupid, Starke? I have security cameras all around the stadium... Yeah, you're alone, and that *is* kinda stupid. There are no other cars in the lot, no cops waiting to bust my ass. You, my nosey friend, are in deep shit." He looked at his goons. "Search him, guys. He could be wearing a wire."

In the second it took them to step up to me, I considered my options. Could I take on two guys who were twice my size? Probably. Could I take them on *and* Tony Paolo? Unlikely.

Which became even clearer, when Sharpie took a small Walther PPK from a desk drawer and pointed it at me. His quarterbacks removed my own handgun, then searched me and took my iPhone.

"No wires," one of them said.

"Can I see that?" Sharpie said. The goon handed him my phone.

He pressed and held a button until the phone turned off. Then he said, "What, you thought I'd break it? Please, stand up."

He tucked the gun away and put on his windbreaker and a baseball cap with the Finley Stadium logo on it.

"What's the plan, Sharpie?" I asked.

"We're taking you for a ride, Harry Starke."

Uh oh. That's not good.

I was about to reply, but there was a sudden blinding white light and an excruciating pain to the back of my head, and then...

23

I came to with a rush. My head was killing me. I could feel my brain throbbing, every beat of my heart pounding on my skull like a hammer on an anvil.

"Ugh, dammit," I muttered, my eyes closed, taking a deep breath. It didn't work.

I opened my eyes but saw only darkness, white stars floating in a firmament of dark matter. I tried to wipe my eyes, but I couldn't move... and then, in one bright flash of insufferable, brilliant white, the lights came on. I tried to turn away, but all I could do was lower my chin to my chest and screw my eyes shut. I was tied down, tight; my hands behind my back, legs to a chair. My butt was sore from the wooden seat, and my shoulders hurt like hell.

"Time to wake up, buddy," someone said, and someone grabbed me by the hair and jerked my head up.

I opened my eyes, the whiteness became a fluorescent light on the ceiling, and I screwed them closed again.

"There he is," another voice said. "Come on, Starke, stay with us, there's a good boy." On some level of my consciousness, I realized the voice belonged to Sharpie

Paolo, but I couldn't quite structure the thought. Had they drugged me? I didn't feel high...

"Screw you," I mumbled.

"That's the spirit!" yet another voice said.

They let go of my hair, and somehow my neck managed to hold up the weight of my head. Slowly, my eyes began to focus, and the light fixture became four long tubes of brilliant white light. *Oh geez!*

And then I began to fully realize the kind of trouble I'd gotten myself into. I was in what looked like an empty warehouse, or maybe a small airplane hangar, or a one-time truck shop. It was a wide, long, open space, empty but for the heaps of garbage piled against the walls, several wooden chairs—one of which I was tied to—and my Maxima, which was parked at the far end of the building, next to one of the rolling steel doors.

My mind was wandering. I couldn't hang on to a single thought for more than a couple of seconds.

I looked up through half-closed eyes. Sharpie's two goons were circling me like a couple of hungry sharks, while the man of the hour stood ten feet away, feet apart, with both his Walther and my M&P9 in his hands. Even in the state I was, I had to smile at the caricature.

"How did you get me out of the stadium?" I asked.

"Carried you to your car, dumbass," one of the quarterbacks said.

"The cameras, surely..." I began saying and trailed off, partly because I needed to swallow, partly because there was no point finishing the sentence.

But Sharpie did anyway, "There's cameras, all right. I turned 'em off. Nobody knows you're here, Starke."

"Where's 'here'?" I asked. "The safe house?"

"One of them. Not that it matters to you, not for much longer anyway," he said as he tucked away both guns.

"I'm gonna need that back," I said.

"The gun?" Sharpie smirked. "You're kidding, right?"

"Sharpie," I said, "you'd better pray I don't get off this chair, because I'm going to break all your fingers one by one."

All three of my captors laughed.

Sharpie said, "Not if you're dead, Starke."

"What are you waiting for, then?"

"Umm... let's call it... a shift change. You'll see. Let's go, boys," he said, and he started for the doors.

As they passed by the Maxima, one of the quarterbacks stopped and kicked in the left headlight.

I mustered all my strength and said, "I owe you a broken leg for that!"

A short laugh rattled in the distance, then a metal door creaked open, letting in daylight, and then it banged shut, leaving me alone.

My hands had been jammed through the back slats of the chair, and then strapped together with a zip tie: I could barely move. Same went for my ankles. They were zip tied to the legs of the chair. I struggled, pushing my upper body back and forth, trying to loosen the chair, but to no avail. Moving my backside from side to side brought more results. The chair began to creak, and then... I lost my frickin' balance and fell sideways, hitting the cement floor with my left shoulder and side of my head, sending new waves of pain through my skull. I had to fight to remain conscious.

I spent the next—it felt like hours—just lying there, breathing slowly, calming myself, dulling the pain, trying to think. One thing I did know: I had to get it together, and quick, because something told me that the next person I saw was going to be the last.

Where could they have taken me? I knew from when Sharpie opened the door, that it was still daylight, but how long I'd been out, I had no idea: It could've been thirty minutes or eight hours, which meant I could've been anywhere from Rock City to New Orleans, though I doubted it was either.

It's quiet outside, I thought, trying to wriggle my fingers, without any luck, *so we're not near any of the major freeways... Not helpful, Harry. You've got to get free from the frickin' chair.*

I struggled some more, trying to free my legs, but the zip ties had all but cut off the blood flow in my legs. I couldn't feel my feet at all, which was a small consolation, but not at all helpful.

It was useless. I could barely move. I looked around. I could try to get to one of the back doors... but then what? I couldn't even bang on them, much less force them open.

It was then that I heard the sound of a car approaching. It stopped. I heard the engine die, then car doors open and close, and men speaking in low voices, too low for me to hear what they were saying. The door opened and five figures, silhouetted against the light, stepped inside: Sharpie, his two goons, and two more, and even silhouetted against the light I knew who they were.

24

"Mr. Starke," Tesak said, his accent thick. "I can't say that I'm happy to see you again, but tell me: how are you feeling?"

They stepped closer, and Brick shielded the light with his wide torso. "Hey, *krisa*," he said.

What the hell he called me, I had no idea, but I figured it wasn't an endearment because he looked like he was about to kick me. I tensed my abdomen. But it didn't happen.

"Relax, Mr. Starke," Tesak said. "We want to talk first." He smiled. To his partner, he said, "*Podnimi yevo.*"

Brick reached down and grabbed the back of the chair with one gorilla-sized hand, set me upright, and stood behind me. I didn't even bother to struggle.

Tony and one of the quarterbacks stepped out, while the other one stood guard at the door. The bastards had handed me over to the Russians.

"I see you're one short," I said. "Paper Boy out doing deliveries?"

"Funny, very funny," Tesak said, standing in front of

me, legs apart, arms folded, head down, looking at me with just the hint of a smile on his lips. "Where we come from, Mr. Starke, they say that as long as a man has his sense of humor, he has hope." He paused for dramatic effect, then said, "It's time we deprived you of your sense of humor."

I knew he wasn't joking when I felt Brick put his hands on my shoulders. They were large and warm, and for one brief shining moment I felt like a kid again, my father's big hands on my shoulders. The feeling didn't last but a second because Tesak took a set of brass knuckles from his pocket and slipped them on. How weird is it; can you believe the only thought I had was, *he's left-handed.*

"Did you break Voron out of prison?" I asked, conversationally, hoping to distract him. It didn't work.

He glanced over my head at Brick. "This one is smart, isn't he? Magnum PI, ah?"

And then, without any further warning, he punched me in the gut, and air blew out of my mouth.

I felt sick, swallowed, and said, "Where is he?"

"Are you interrogating me, Mr. Starke?" Tesak said and delivered another punch.

My ribs didn't crack, thank God.

I said, "Why'd you start shooting at the Sorbonne? Because of Voron?"

Tesak was already breathing hard—he would be turning seventy next autumn, so he'd said in the bar that night, and he wasn't in the best of shape.

"Had to follow the plan," he said, leaning forward and resting his hands on his knees.

"Even at the cost of Paper Boy's life?" I asked, catching my own breath and getting ready for the next gut-punch.

"Voron is our brother, Mr. Starke. We will die for our brothers."

"I'm guessing you will," I said, and then Tesak punched me in the face.

I rocked back in the chair, but Brick was there to support me. How nice of him. I felt around my mouth with my tongue, made sure my teeth were all still there, and spat blood. Thank the Lord, Tesak's strength was proportional to his age... and size.

"I want you to know, Mr. Starke," Tesak said, "that I take no pleasure in this. I am simply avenging my friend."

"That's a bit grandiose, isn't it?"

Another punch, this time on a cheek, and I had no choice but to turn the other one... Actually, Brick turned it for me. I could tell that Tesak was running out of breath, and I hoped to hell they weren't about to switch roles. I guessed the smaller man wanted to draw blood, and then the gorilla behind me would finish the job.

"You know the feds are involved, right?" I said, more hopefully than I felt. "You're not going to get away with this."

"We know, Mr. Starke," Tesak said, and he punched me again. "But our work is done. Our debt to Voron is paid."

"Your debt?" I asked to keep him talking.

"Doesn't matter now."

"The cops will be here soon," I said, more to myself than to the Russians.

"*Nyet*! They will not," Brick bellowed.

And everything stopped at the sound of gunfire outside.

Tesak turned. I could tell it was only one gun that was doing the shooting, which made it unlikely the CPD had come to the rescue. Who, then?

The quarterback at the door was in no hurry to find out, but he was listening. Muffled voices, incoherent shouting, came from the outside, followed by even louder noises. I thought I heard bones crack, but in retrospect that really wasn't possible. Suddenly, the door flew open with a crash, hitting the quarterback on the face, hard. He flew backward, holding his nose; it was already streaming blood.

A shape jumped through the door, pistol raised.

"Stay on the ground!" the man shouted.

The quarterback raised his hands, as blood ran down his face. He was shaking.

Tesak also raised his hands but hadn't taken off the brass knuckles.

The shape pointed the gun at the guy on the floor, and said, "Get out. Run, if you know what's good for you."

The quarterback crawled to the door and scurried away, and the four of us listened to his footsteps on the gravel as he ran away.

The man, silhouetted against the light streaming in through the door, was aiming his gun at Tesak, who stood motionless, his hands in the air.

"Who.... are you?" Tesak asked.

"None of your business," the shape said as it stepped closer.

The man looked familiar—over six feet and built like a refrigerator—but my aching mind couldn't quite place the face.

"But it is my business," Tesak argued.

I felt Brick shifting behind me, and I almost wanted to tell him not to try anything. Almost.

Everything happened very fast after that. Tesak lowered his hands a little too quickly to the shape's liking, and Brick reached for a gun tucked in his pants. But the shape must have had some serious training, because his gun swung toward Brick even before his eyes shifted, and he let out two quick shots—the classic double-tap.

Brick crashed to the floor like a pile of... bricks—no pun intended.

Tesak twitched but didn't turn to look.

The shape leaped toward him and tapped him on the temple with the butt of his gun. Tesak went down, brass knuckles jangling on the cement floor.

The whole thing took maybe two seconds, which sounds like no time at all, but for a trained professional like this guy obviously was, two seconds was more than enough.

He kneeled down and checked Tesak's pulse, then stepped around my chair and did the same with Brick.

"Damn," he muttered.

"Dead?" I asked.

"Oh yeah."

He walked back around, and I saw my Smith & Wesson in his hand.

"Is that my gun?" I said.

He glanced at it. "Yeah, I suppose it is."

"Where have we met?" I asked, studying the man's face.

"The Sorbonne," he said. "I was the guy staring at you through the mirror."

It clicked. Of course, it was him, the ex-military guy.

"What the hell are you doing here?" I asked.

"I could ask you the same question."

"I'm on a case."

He looked around. "You are, huh? How's it going?" he asked, with a sarcastic grin on his face.

"Are you going to untie me or what?" I asked. "And what's your name, anyway?"

"I'll untie you, Starke," he said. "But just give me a minute. It's safer for you to stay right where you are for just a little longer. Safer for me, too."

"Huh?"

"Last time we met, you were going to beat the shit out of me, weren't you?" he grinned. "Yeah, I've been in a bar fight or two in my time, and I know that look. Most guys like to hold eye contact before a fight. Those guys usually lose."

"What's your point?" I asked.

"You were staring at my chest? Or maybe it was my throat? Either way, Starke, I figured you were probably about to kick my ass, I saw it in your eyes. I guess I was lucky these assholes decided the Sorbonne was the next best thing to the OK Corral."

I didn't believe a word of it. If I was right, the guy was ex-special forces and more than capable of handling little old me. Hell, he'd just proved it.

"THEY SHOT A COP," I said.

"They grazed him, from what I've seen in the media, and one of them died for it. One less to deal with here, right?"

My hands were sore, as were my legs, but I was too tired to protest. The man winked and then turned around to leave.

"Where the hell are you going?" I yelled after him.

"Gotta clear the perimeter, Starke. I'll be right back."

He tucked my gun into his waistband behind his back, walked to the door, opened it, and then turned to me, and said, "And my name's Bob Ryan—"

I don't know if he was going to add to the statement because someone smacked him on the back of his head with what looked like, and sounded like, a piece of iron pipe. Bob Ryan fell face-first to the floor, unconscious.

25

W ell, crap. *Why didn't the stupid SOB untie me before he went to "clear the perimeter"?*
Yes, that's right, one of my first interactions with Bob Ryan was seeing him crash comically, like a sack of potatoes, to the cement floor of an abandoned warehouse.

His fall echoed around the big open space, and then yet another silhouette filled the door frame. I could see, even from where I was, that he was a much smaller, older man. He stood for a second, looking down at Ryan, then lowered his weapon.

I couldn't see his face or any other features, but I knew instinctively it was Voron. He stepped inside, looked around, and then he shut the door.

"Voron?" I yelled.

No answer. The figure, now dark in the dimness, leaned over Ryan's body, reached down and picked up the gun—my gun. He checked it, weighed it in his hand.

"Your friend will be all right, Mr. Starke," Voron said.

"He's not my friend," I barked and then spat blood.

"I'm sorry if my friends hurt you," he said as he walked stiffly toward me.

All those years in prison have taken their toll.

He held the pipe in one hand and my gun in the other, pointed downward toward the floor, and I was relieved to see his finger was not on the trigger. His white hair was tied back in a ponytail. He was wearing a black, long-sleeve T-shirt and baggy tan pants.

"Is Brick dead?" he asked quietly.

"I'd say so." I could smell copper in the air.

"Pity. At least Tesak is still breathing."

Voron stopped next to Tesak's body. The old man on the floor was still breathing, but there was a nasty gash on his temple.

"You here to finish the job?" I asked, glancing at my gun in his hand.

Voron raised it slightly, glanced down at it. "With this? Not at all. Not my method, as you know." He raised the pipe then. "This, on the other hand... maybe."

"Then you'd better get on with it," I said jadedly. "My hands are killing me."

I wasn't lying, either. My hands had gone numb, and the rest of my body could use a good Thai massage. I swallowed, stared at the man, awaiting his next move.

He said, "That's not why I'm here, Mr. Starke."

"Oh, yeah? Then why *are* you here?" I said. "Why the hell are you in Chattanooga?"

"To meet with old friends, nothing more," he said in a quiet voice.

"And then what?" I pressed. "Kill Jim McDowell?"

"No. I don't want any trouble."

"I'd say it's a little late for that, Voron."

A smile touched his thin lips. "If I wanted someone dead, Mr. Starke, they'd be dead already."

He pointed the gun at my chest, his hand steady, and then lowered it again.

Point taken.

I said, "So, are you going to untie me, give me back my gun?"

"No. That I cannot do. I have matters to attend to, and I need all the head start I can get, you understand."

Voron looked around, as I sat there panting, angry beyond words, but I was helpless. The killer used his shirt-tail to wipe the gun clean, and then he put it down on the floor a few feet away from me.

"So, that's it then?" I asked. "You're going to leave me here and just disappear into the night? That's the plan? You know the feds are on your tail, right? Every cop in the state is looking for you."

"And yet, here I am. I have made my way from Nashville to Chattanooga, and you never suspected a thing."

I couldn't argue with that.

I said, "Will we be seeing you again, Voron? I have some questions, whenever you have the time."

The ex-assassin smirked. "Most certainly, Mr. Starke. Sooner than you think."

He gave me a slight nod, which I guessed was his way of saying goodbye, and then he dropped the pipe and walked to the exit, stepping over Bob Ryan and then out into the daylight.

There was a moment's pause, and then I heard a car engine start, and then it was gone.

Finally, I could relax, let my body slump in the chair,

my head fall forward on my chest. I spat on the floor between my legs, sucking in deep breaths, feeling every cut bleeding and every bruise pushing its way to the surface. I flexed my fingers, trying to keep the blood flowing. All I could do now was hope Ryan would wake up before Tesak.

I closed my eyes and drifted...

26

I awoke with a jerk. Someone was shaking me. "Come on, wake up!" The voice sounded annoyed.

I opened my eyes a little, sniffed, squinted, saw the man's boots.

And then someone slapped me once, twice.

"Come on, Starke, wake up. That's it, easy now," Bob Ryan said. "Hold up. Can you sit up straight?"

I closed my eyes again; the overhead light was too bright, but I did lean back, holding steady. Then I opened my eyes slightly to see what was happening. Ryan knelt down, opened a small Swiss Army knife, and cut the zip ties. Slowly, I tried to straighten my legs. They felt as if... nothing. It was as if I didn't own them.

Ryan stepped around behind the chair.

"How long have I been here?" I asked.

"When did they bring you?"

"Morning, sometime after eleven, maybe. What time is it now?"

"Three in the afternoon."

"Damn..."

"You got that right, buddy."

The zip tie behind my back snapped, but my hands stayed where they were; I couldn't move them. My shoulders had locked; the pain in my joints was excruciating. I took a deep breath, then slowly extricated my hands from between the slats and brought my arms forward, making circular motions with my shoulders.

"Better?" he asked.

I nodded, winced as spears of pain shot through my arms, hands, and fingers.

I looked around. Tesak was still out cold, and my gun was lying next to him. I could smell blood in the air. I looked around at Brick, more excruciating pain.

"Yeah," Ryan said, "the big guy's dead."

"No huge loss," I said.

"Asked for it, didn't he?" Ryan said.

I watched as he searched through Brick's jacket pockets, then his pants pockets. He found the man's wallet and revolver. He tossed the wallet aside and tucked the gun into his own pants pocket.

"How's your head?" I asked.

"Been better, been worse." He stood up. "So, you saw the guy who jumped me?"

"Yeah. Vlad Voronov, the Raven," I said.

Ryan frowned. I didn't know it then, but I'd become very familiar with that frown in the years to follow.

"Voron?" he said. "What the hell was he doing here?"

I twisted in the chair, then unsteadily stood up and stretched my legs; I was in frickin' agony as my muscles protested.

"I could ask you the same question," I said. "What are you doing here? Were you following me? Or them?"

"Neither. I was about to go into Peeky's on Chestnut for a late breakfast when I saw you go into the stadium offices." He smiled, then said, "I was kinda intrigued, so I continued to watch, and fifteen minutes later I saw them drag you out... So I followed them."

"You took your frickin' time getting in here. The bastards almost killed me."

"Yes, sorry about that... Look, I'm good, but not that good. There were five of them, right? I had to pick my moment."

"Why were you at the Sorbonne that night, Ryan?"

He stood on the other side of the chair, and I kept my eyes on his. He smiled, raised his hands slightly, showing he wasn't going to start anything. I picked up my pistol.

"Believe it or not," he said, "I was just having a drink."

"Is that so?" I said. "Two times I run into you, under extraordinary circumstances, someone I've never met before... and now here you are. That's one hell of a coincidence, don't you think?"

He simply shrugged. I continued to look him in the eye, holding his gaze, he didn't flinch, *impressive!*

I nodded, slowly, not really convinced, but he struck me as a guy who wasn't into playing games. I didn't fully trust him, but I wasn't sensing any BS, either.

"I suppose," he said finally. "Wrong time, wrong place, huh? Two times? I guess you're a lucky guy."

"You could say that," I said. "Thanks for getting me out of this mess."

"You're welcome."

I tucked my Smith & Wesson into my waistband. The Russian bastards had stripped me of my jacket and shoulder-holster.

I extended my hand. "Harry Starke," I said. "Nice to properly meet you."

He shook my hand. "Bob Ryan. What now?"

"I need to find my phone," I said and headed for my car on legs that would barely hold me up.

"What do you want me to do with this asshole?" Ryan asked, pointing at Tesak.

"Tie him up? Use his shirt or something."

"There are two more outside. A big guy and a small one."

I rolled my eyes. "Hah! No shit... Let me get my phone, then we'll take care of it."

My car was unlocked, and I was glad to find my jacket and holster in the driver's seat. I figured they must've been planning to torch the car when they were done with me—what was left of me—inside it. I donned the holster, slipped into my jacket, and holstered my gun. That done, I began to feel a little better. I did a couple of squats and almost passed out again.

Damn, that hurts.

Ryan had propped Tesak on the chair but hadn't restrained him. I stepped outside. The sun blinded me momentarily, but my eyes adjusted quickly, and I found myself in the parking lot of a warehouse building with rolling metal doors at intervals as far as the eye could see. The lot was empty and overgrown in places, clearly abandoned, and surrounded by a wire fence, and I knew where I was.

It has since been demolished, but back then, before Volkswagen came to town, the area was called Hangar Town—a labyrinth of warehouses and prefabricated office buildings, all meant to revitalize the city's economy. Unfortunately, delay after delay slowed construction almost to a stop and by the time the infrastructure was complete, what few businesses that had been on board had pulled out, and the developer had gone broke. Hangar Town became a ghost town.

Sharpie Paolo was sprawled on his back on the asphalt. The remaining quarterback was propped against the wall. Both were unconscious, but breathing, which was good: one body was better than three, though I doubted Kate would see it that way.

I knelt down beside Sharpie—the muscles in my legs and hips still complaining—and rummaged through his windbreaker until I found my phone. I turned it on and waited for what seemed to be an interminably long time for the screen to open and find a signal. When it did, I was bombarded with messages and missed calls, most of them from Tim, Ronnie, and Jacque, but some from Kate and even my father.

I responded to Kate first.

"Harry?" she said. "Where have you been? Where are you?"

"Long story. I'll tell you when you get here," I replied.

"Get where? What's going on?"

"Hangar Town. Come on, Kate. Get your ass in gear."

"Why? What the hell are you doing there?"

"You'll see when you get here," I said. "And Kate? Consider this a nine-one-one call. We have a body and three suspects in custody."

"*What?* Geez, Harry. Okay. I'm on my way. Who's 'we' this time?"

"Just come on down here as soon as you can. I gotta go."

I clicked off and put the phone away. Fully expecting Ryan to have disappeared, I stepped back into the warehouse.

"How'd it go?" he asked as he finished tying up Tesak.

"The police are on their way."

He gave a short nod. "Good. D'you need help with the two guys outside?"

"Yeah. Let's go."

Bob Ryan has always been hard to crack, but that day, our first interactions were the toughest. I could *not* get a read on him.

"So, tell me again, how did you find me?" I asked when we were out in the parking lot.

He stepped up to the quarterback and said, "And I told you I wasn't looking for you." He grabbed the quarterback by the hands and dragged him to the door.

I did the same with Sharpie, though I wished to hell I hadn't.

"You followed them?" I asked.

"That's right. The muscle flung you into the back seat of your car and took off fast. That little shit," he said and nodded at Sharpie, "followed. I followed them."

"And they didn't spot you?" I asked.

"What's with you, Starke? No, they didn't spot me, obviously... Look, I'm more than familiar with the art of tailing a suspect, okay?"

"You're a cop?" I asked. It was my turn to hold the door for him, as he shoved the hefty quarterback through the door.

"I used to be. Chicago PD. I'm also a Marine."

I frowned. "Ex-Marine?"

"There's no such thing; you should know that," he said, with a smile. "Semper Fi, right? Ooh ra!"

I did know, but I wanted to be sure he did. "I used to be a cop too," I said. "Chattanooga PD."

"I know," he smiled. "I asked around."

I had to smile at that.

"So, you followed the Russians when they left the Sorbonne. Where did they go?" I asked.

We dropped Sharpie and his henchman next to the chair, at Tesak's feet. All three men were still out cold, but I knew they wouldn't be for much longer.

"They camped out here that night," Ryan said, "but they were gone the next morning. My guess is to break out their pal Voron."

"That's the theory. Who drove them?"

"There's a whole fleet of cars in one of these buildings. I've seen this back in Chicago. They steal cars, brand them with new VIN numbers, forge papers. A real *Gone In 60 Seconds* operation."

"Sounds like Sharpie's work to me," I said.

"That the small guy?"

"Yeah. Tony Paolo. We've been trying to bust him for years."

"You can thank me later," Ryan said.

We stood around for a minute, and then I said, "Why'd you do it?"

"What do you mean?" he asked.

"There were other people in the bar that night, but none of them decided to follow the shooters. Why'd you do it?"

Ryan appeared to be considering the question, and then he shrugged. He said, "Don't know. Old instincts die hard, I suppose. I saw them shooting and... well, you know how it goes. I'm sure you can relate."

I could. In fact, it was largely the driving force behind my decision to leave the CPD. Office politics and bureaucracy getting in the way of the job, taking down the bad guys. I nodded.

"So," Ryan said, "where does that leave us?"

I knew where he was going with that. Kate would be here any minute, and she'd be bringing half of the CPD with her. They'd be finding me, all beat up, along with an ex-Chicago cop who'd just shot Brick twice in the chest... with my gun.

Geez, that's terrific. I wonder how that's going to go down?

I needed to know what Ryan's game was. The answer to my next question would tell me a lot about the guy and his motivations.

"What d'you think I should tell them?" I asked.

"We better tie these guys up," he said, dodging the question.

He took off Sharpie's windbreaker, and then I helped him carry Tesak and the chair to one side, some ten feet away from Brick's body, and we used strips of Sharpie's jacket to tie the three men together by their hands.

"Well," I said, finally, "are you going to answer my question?"

Ryan turned to me and said, "I think we should come clean."

I held his gaze, waiting for more.

"You tell them exactly what happened, how they got you here, Voron, me, the whole story. Then, I'll tell them, well, everything... I take it we're not going after Voron, then?"

"We? We're not going anywhere," I said.

"Then, my job here is done. I'll come clean to the cops, claim self-defense, that I was in fear for my life, and yours. You'll back me up. Shouldn't be a problem."

"No," I said, shaking my head.

"No? What do you mean 'no'? If you want me to run,

you can forget it, Starke. If I hadn't done what I did, you'd be dead right now. I'll tell the truth and take my chances. You tell 'em whatever the hell you like."

I had one of those feelings again, like something wasn't quite right. Or, rather, that I needed to intervene to keep things together, whatever that meant. There were still questions to which I needed answers, questions which Ryan had danced around.

"I don't want you to run, but it wouldn't be a good idea to tell them the whole truth and nothing by the truth."

"Why the hell not?" he asked. "I just got here, Starke. The last thing I need is to get on the CPD's bad side."

"And what brought you here, exactly?" I asked in turn.

"Sightseeing," he lied.

I'd heard the lie before, from Paper Boy.

"We need a cover story," I persisted. "I'll trust you, Ryan, for now, but they won't. An ex-Chicago cop shows up in Chattanooga and takes down a couple of Russian killers? That raises too many questions. How the hell are you going to explain it? Kate Gazzara doesn't believe in coincidence any more than I do. You think she'll just let you walk? Forget it. We'll do it my way."

He was quiet for a long moment, and then he said, "Fair enough, Starke. Any idea what the cover story might be?"

"A couple, but you'll have to follow my lead."

"And if I don't?"

I took a breath. "Then, you're on your own, pal, and I can't help you."

Outside, police sirens wailed.

27

"And what exactly are you going to help me with, Starke?" Ryan asked. There was no aggression in his voice, merely curiosity, as if we were negotiating some kind of deal, and he wanted to hear more about what I had to offer.

"That depends on you, Ryan," I said, "and on what you tell me once we're done with these three."

"These four, you mean," he said, jerking his head at Brick's body.

"Right. Well? Are we on?"

The sirens were getting closer. Any minute now, cops would burst in.

"Okay," he said, "you win. I'll follow your lead."

"Good."

"But if I think you're messing up, Starke, I'll say so."

"Look, I can handle Kate... Sergeant Gazzara, but I can't vouch for the rest of them, so just keep your mouth shut."

He frowned at that. "Again, what do you have in mind?" he asked.

"You'll see."

"That's hardly—"

Kate stormed in through the front door.

"Hands in the air!" she shouted.

She was pointing her gun at us, as were three more uniformed officers behind her. Ryan and I both had our hands in the air, and we stepped aside for the cops to see our restrained suspects.

"Kate!" I called. "It's all right. It's me. All clear."

Kate signaled to the other officers to check out the perimeter.

"We could use some handcuffs here, guys," I said.

"Hands where I can see them," she said, pointing her gun at Ryan, who already had his hands up.

"That's unnecessary, Kate," I said.

She glared at me, then back at Ryan, then said, "And who the hell are you?"

"My name's Bob Ryan," he said as more cops entered the building and surrounded us.

"He's with me, Kate," I said.

She slowly lowered her weapon and signaled for the others to do the same. They did.

She said, "Surrender your weapons, both of you."

I took mine from its holster, and Ryan carefully produced the revolver he'd taken from Brick's cold dead hand.

Hmm. Where have I heard that before?

We handed them to one of the officers, who bagged them and took them away.

"Geez, Harry," Kate said, "you look like you've been hit by a truck. You need a doctor!"

"Maybe later," I said. "Let's deal with this situation first."

Kate glanced at the tied-up trio. "Whoa... Is that?"

"It is indeed," I said, lightly. "Tesak himself. Brick, over there, wasn't so lucky, though."

"Forensics will be here shortly," Kate said. "Let's move this outside."

One of the officers had rolled open one of the doors. I glanced at the broken headlight as we walked past my Maxima out into the open. Had it not been for the presence of Kate and her team, I would have gone back inside and kicked the crap out of the remaining quarterback.

Kate paused, turned, and crossed her arms over her chest. "Okay, I'm listening."

Ryan glanced at me.

I said, "Kate Gazzara, meet Bob Ryan, my intern."

Ryan cleared his throat loudly and then smiled at Kate and put out his hand. She shook it, a little reluctantly.

"Intern?" she asked. "You're kidding, right? He's old enough to be your brother."

"Just started," Ryan said. "This was my first assign-ment." He grinned at her.

She turned to me and said, "You really are full of crap, Harry. Okay, let's start at the top, shall we?"

I took a deep breath, and then told Kate what had happened to me over the previous two days, sparing no detail about Sharpie and his operation, or at least what I knew of it.

Kate nodded and then asked Ryan, "What about you?"

"We actually met at the Sorbonne," I answered for him, "the night of the shooting."

"Is that so?" Kate asked.

"Yup," Ryan confirmed.

"Ryan here is also an ex-cop, from Chicago. We hit it off, and he told me he was looking for work. I figured I could use another field agent. Turned out, I was right. Ryan saved my ass today."

"Thank you, Mr. Ryan," Kate said. "But, just to be clear, you did shoot the guy in there, right?"

"I had to, I'm afraid," Ryan said. "They were torturing Harry, so I had to intervene. I entered the building; the big guy drew his weapon. I was in fear for my life, and for Harry's. I responded accordingly."

Wow, good answer, Bob.

"Very efficient," she said dryly.

We spent the next twenty minutes explaining our movements, and to Ryan's credit, he improvised well. Kate, for the most part, seemed to buy it, although I knew she'd have questions for me later. Like why I'd never mentioned Ryan to her.

But that was for later. Right now, I had to get moving.

"You look impatient, Harry," Kate said. "I think you should slow down and get your face looked at. It's a mess."

Ryan chuckled.

"Why, thank you, Kate," I said sarcastically. "You also look great." The difference was, she really did look great, and I could see Ryan actively appraising her.

She smiled, then she said, "I'm serious, Harry. Come on, let's go. I need to take your official statements."

Kate gave orders to the rest of her team, and then Ryan and I sat in the back seat of her cruiser for the ride to Amnicola. Our cars had become part of the crime scene.

28

W e arrived at the Police Service Center on Amnicola at around four-thirty that afternoon. We followed Kate inside, to the interview rooms, where we found Assistant Chief Henry Finkle waiting for us.

"My God, what have you done now, Starke?" he barked.

"Take it easy, Henry," I said.

"Oh, I'm trying to, but every time I see you, there are bodies piling up behind you."

"Just one body, actually," Ryan said.

"Holy... so now that's two!" Finkle turned to Kate and said, "Gazzara, maybe you can tell me what the hell's going on?"

"Not yet, Henry, but give me a little time..." she let it trail off.

He shook his head, then nodded, then glared at me, then at Ryan. "For God's sake, sort it out, Sergeant." Then he turned and stomped away.

I grinned at Ryan. Ryan stared stoically back at me. *Does the guy not have a frickin' sense of humor, or what?*

They separated us into adjoining interview rooms and Kate took my statement and two hours later turned me loose... sort of.

She led me out into the corridor and said, "Is there something you're not telling me, Harry?"

"Yes," I said truthfully.

She shook her head, slowly, looked into my eyes, and said, "Damn you, Harry Starke. I know that look. You're close to cracking it, right?" she asked.

"Yes, maybe... I think so, but there are a few things I need to confirm first."

"Do you know where Voron is?" she asked.

"I don't, but I soon might."

"Did he kill Sandra McDowell?"

"I'll be sure to ask him, Kate. Do you need me for anything else? I have to go and save the day." I smiled and flinched as my split lip cracked.

She took me to an empty side room where others couldn't see us, and she put a hand on my cheek. She said, "I know you're not going to listen to me, but, please, Harry, don't get yourself killed."

"That's one thing I will listen to, Kate, I promise," I said, and I kissed her.

We held each other tightly for a long moment, and then she let go.

She said, "I'm serious, Harry. Call me if you need me. No, call me anyway. I can get you and your *intern* off the hook with this Sharpie thing and the dead Russian, but Finkle is fit to be tied about Voronov. He's wanting answers like, yesterday. And if he gets it into his head that you're holding out... well, I don't know what he'll do."

"Don't worry," I said. "It won't be long now. Just a few loose ends," I lied.

The truth was, I did have a sort of half-assed theory, but there were a lot of things I wasn't sure of. I had little time to confirm—or refute—them so I had to act fast.

"Where are you headed?" Kate asked.

"I haven't decided yet. Probably to the office."

That wasn't true either. I knew exactly where I was going, and it wasn't my office.

"Okay," she said. "Do you need anything else?"

"I don't suppose you'll let me take my gun?" I asked, knowing the answer.

"It's evidence," Kate said.

"Of course."

I felt naked without my trusty Smith & Wesson, but I couldn't argue with police procedure.

"Well, I guess I'd better get out of here," I said. "You'll let me know if Ryan's not who he says he is?" I grinned, but Kate didn't. I said, "Okay, with your permission, ma'am, I'll leave."

And I did.

I called for an Uber and went outside to wait. I needed a car in the worst way. I looked at my watch.

"Damn," I mumbled. "It's already after seven. No chance now, I bet."

I was wrong. I made a call and then had the Uber driver take me to a small used car lot on Brainerd Road where I happened to know the owner, Kenny "The Rake" Cassell. There I purchased a high-mileage, 2001 Ford Explorer Sport Trac for eleven grand on a promise that I'd have Ronnie write the man a check and deliver it in the morning, and I drove off with a temporary tag in the back window. By the time I got out of there, it was almost eight.

I called Tim. He answered after the first ring.

"Harry? Are you all right?" he said, and then someone grabbed the phone from him.

"You 'kay, boss?" Jacque asked.

"I'm all right. I'm fine..."

Ronnie grabbed the phone then and put it on speaker. He said, "Where the hell are you, man? What the hell happened?"

It took some explaining, and I did my best to tell the whole truth and nothing but the truth, and my team took it really well.

"So, you're coming to work?" Jacque asked.

Then it hit me: "Work?" I said. "It's after eight o'clock. What are you guys still doing at the office?"

Ronnie chuckled. "Oh, we aren't at the office, man! I'm sipping on a twenty-two-ounce beer at the bar."

"I'm having an appletini," Jacque chimed in.

"I'm having a root beer," Tim said.

"Well, good for y'all," I replied. "Tim, do you have a pen on you?"

"I have my iPad," he said.

"Can you take notes?"

"Of course."

"Take this down. Robert Ryan, mid-thirties. Ex-Marine —yeah, I know there's no such thing as an ex-Marine; choke on it—he's also an ex-cop with Chicago PD, at least, that's what he told me. Can you check him out?"

"Consider it done," Tim said, eager to get to work.

"What did you find out about Mary Turner?" I asked, hoping to get all of my questions answered then and there.

I didn't.

"I've tracked down the person who tagged Mary's files. He's actually quite a famous hacker, calls himself MegaBear—"

"Mega Bear?" I asked.

"MegaBear007, actually, all one word. I tracked him down, but he—maybe it's a she—anyway, he's not talking. As in—the moment I reached out, he blocked my access. I can no longer even search for him, Harry, and I'm afraid if I do, he might just fry our system."

"Damn it... Did you learn anything?"

"Not much. Mary Turner is definitely a fake identity."

"That's all I needed to know, Tim," I said. "Thank you. You can drop her for now. We don't want all those expensive toys to be destroyed, do we?"

"We do not!" Tim said.

"All right, guys, I gotta run. Tim, your priority is Ryan. I'll check in tomorrow morning. This time I really am going to show up."

"You'd better," Ronnie said.

"Miss ya, boss," Jacque said.

"Enough, you," I said, and I clicked off.

I had to admit, I missed them too. Being out of the office so much over the past few days made me feel like I was on a very busy, very dangerous roller-coaster. I'd been shot at, kidnapped, beaten half to death... It was time to finish it.

Mary Turner had been on my mind every step of the way, and I was pretty sure I now knew who she really was. What I didn't know was how, if at all, she was connected to Sandra McDowell's murder. Which is why my first stop was Jim McDowell's house. I knew damn well the man had been hiding something from me and the CPD, but not for much longer. I only hoped that Voron hadn't beaten me to it.

As I approached the iron gates at Jim's mansion, my optimism wavered: the gates stood open. I pulled up to the electronic box and pushed the button: nothing.

I floored the gas pedal and the Sport Trac flew up the driveway and skidded to a stop at the bottom of the front steps.

I jumped out of the car and ran up the steps. The door was wide open. I stepped inside, reached for my weapon. My holster was empty. *Crap! Now what?*

"Jim?" I shouted. "It's Harry Starke."

There was a moment of silence, and then I heard Jim say, "Harry?"

His voice sounded weak and came from somewhere deep within the massive house.

"Where are you?" I called.

"Back patio, Harry."

I rushed through the house and out the back, and I found Jim slumped in a wicker chair by the pool. The sky-blue water danced, the underwater lights painting the patio in flickering sapphire.

Jim was in a bad way. His nose was surely broken, his right eyebrow split, and a streak of blood had run down his face and stained the front of his shirt.

"Harry?" he said, his eyes blinking, trying to focus on me. "They... they took her. They took Chelsea!"

Damn it! I'm too late.

"I'm here now, Jim. Who took her? Who did this to you? Was it Voron?"

"No, not Voron. Two men, about your age. They were dressed in dark clothes, cheap. Mobsters, I'm sure. They had prison tattoos on their hands... Harry, how could I have allowed this to happen? I should've reported everything."

I wanted to agree with him, but now wasn't the right time. He seemed to be reasonably stable, so I pressed him.

"What else did you see, Jim?" I asked. "Come on, damn it. Tell me. We don't have much time."

"They came in two trucks. I saw them through the security cameras at the gate."

"Can you describe the trucks?"

He closed his eyes, focused, and then he said, "One was a big Detroit SUV, maybe a Tahoe or a Yukon. The other was smaller, but..."

"Stay with me, Jim. But what?"

"It was smaller... with big wheels. One of those loud monster trucks kids drive. Like a..."

"Like a Jeep Wrangler?" I asked, my mind racing.

"Yes. Yes, exactly. Does that help?"

"More than you know," I said. "How long ago did they leave?"

He shook his head, trying to focus his thoughts. He coughed. Blood spurted from his nose. I thought he was going to pass out, but he didn't.

"Fifteen, twenty minutes. No more than that."

I nodded. "I'll get Chelsea back, Jim, I promise. Now, I need you to call 911 and stay put until they get here. Can you do that?"

He nodded. He was still disoriented, but he sat up straight in the chair and looked around. He didn't speak, but his eyes were focused.

I helped him up and then took him inside the house. He sat down on a sofa in the hall while I did a quick check of the house and locked all the doors.

I said, "Call the cops, Jim, and an ambulance. I have to go."

He picked up a cell phone from the hall table and looked up at me.

"Where did they take my girl?" he asked, his shoulders slumped.

"I'm going to find out." I looked down at him. "And when I get back, you're going to tell me all about Mary Turner. Deal?"

"Whatever you say, Harry."

"One last thing," I said. "Do you have any guns in the house? I need one."

Jim set the phone down on the table, rose unsteadily to his feet, went to a small door under the main staircase, opened the door, and went inside. He returned a moment later with a shiny old 1895 model Frontier Colt .45 six-shooter and a small box of bullets.

"Nice," I said as I hefted the single-action revolver, wondering what would happen if I had to fire it, whether or not it would blow my frickin' hand off.

I loaded the weapon, leaving one chamber empty for the hammer, and put the rest of the bullets in my jacket pocket. Then I patted Jim on the shoulder and rushed outside and remounted the Sport Trac.

It was dark, the air cool, the night was quiet. Jim's driveway was illuminated by old-fashioned streetlamps that made it look like a path in a national park.

Gravel flew from under my wheels as I turned the car around and drove out of the open gates and turned right. I didn't pay it any attention, but I did notice a large black SUV parked at the side of the road facing the other direction.

30

I turned right past the SUV and floored it down the road.

"Siri, call Tim," I said into my iPhone, and she did.

"I'm back at the office," he said when he picked up after the first ring, "but I haven't found anything bad about Ryan yet. He was a cop and—"

"Tim," I said, interrupting him. "I need you to drop what you're doing and concentrate, okay? Remember the guy who had the DUI? Drives a custom Wrangler?"

"The Provost's son? Sure do. Richard Mason."

"Can you find him? Right now?"

Damn these inconsiderate SOBs. Dim your friggin' headlights, asshole. It was at times like that, I missed the blue lights and the sirens.

I heard Tim typing furiously. He said, "Working on it, Harry. Give me a minute, okay?"

He clicked off before I could reply.

Dammit. I slowed down and watched the road, thinking, as cars passed by in the opposite direction, blinding me with their headlights.

I was going nowhere fast—literally. So, I pulled over and waited, and I had a thought: I called another number.

"Kate?" I said, trying to sound calm and collected.

"Hey, Harry," she said brightly. "Have you solved it yet?" I detected a hint of sarcasm in the question.

"I might have, in fact... No, listen, is Bob Ryan still there?"

"Yeah. We've taken a break. Ryan is getting coffee in the lounge."

"Can I speak to him, please?" I asked.

"What? You don't have your intern's phone number?"

I was quiet for a moment, then said, "Of course I do. But didn't you take his phone?"

"I don't think so. Anyway, here he is. Hey, Ryan. It's Harry. He wants to talk to you."

"Hey, Harry. What's up?" he said.

"Bob. Can you hear me okay?" I asked in a low voice.

"Er... Yeah."

"Can Kate?"

There was a pause, and then he said, "No. What's going on?"

"I have a situation, Bob. Jim McDowell's daughter, Chelsea, has been kidnapped."

"McDowell. The guy whose wife was murdered, right?"

"That's the one."

I gave Ryan a quick, bare-bones version of the events, as well as my theory about who was behind it. He listened without interruption, then took a minute to think it over.

He said, "Makes sense to me. What do you need?"

"Call me back on this number when the CPD is done with you. I'm thinking I'm going to need some backup."

"Got it."

My phone vibrated with another call. I said, "Got another call coming in. Good luck, Bob."

"Thanks."

I switched lines and said, "Tim?"

"I found our Jeep, Harry. I pinged Mason's phone. He's at his mother's home; the car's parked out front. I'm looking at it right now."

"Talk to me," I said. "Tell me about the geography of the place and its security."

And he did, in detail, as seen from the satellites. The property wasn't as big as the McDowell mansion, but that was actually a disadvantage—it would be tough to infiltrate, especially considering the security system: mainly cameras outside and a fairly sophisticated alarm system inside.

"Can you kill the cameras?"

Tim thought about it, then said, "I could, but that would alert them. I have a better idea."

"Tell me."

"It looks like there are a couple of blind spots on the perimeter wall and the house itself. I'll use the cameras to guide you safely to the back door, and then I can deactivate the house alarm. You can then turn off the cameras once you're inside."

"Are there any cameras inside?" I said.

"If there are, they're not being monitored, but that's not the point: they'll only be watching the outside. People don't expect danger from within, only from without. Once you're inside, you're home free, so long as you don't make a sound, and—"

"Okay, Tim," I said, interrupting him. "Give me a minute."

I thought it over. I wasn't too happy about having to

dodge the cameras, but I couldn't think of anything better. It would have to do.

"Not bad, kid," I said. "Where'd you learn all that?"

"*Splinter Cell*," he said proudly.

"Oh, yeah, I love those books."

"Books?" Tim asked.

"Never mind. Tell me about Mason's son."

Made sense to know my enemies, right?

"Okay," Tim said, "I'm looking at his sheet. He looks like a typical bully, Harry; big, ugly, mean, dumb. I've been dogged by idiots like him all through my youth." I could hear the contempt in his voice.

Your youth? Hell, Tim, you're only seventeen now.

"Richard Mason," Tim continued, "thirty-two. Played football at Chattanooga Central High School, currently unemployed. One arrest in September 2007 for DUI. His alcohol level was point-150. He must have been wasted. He was sentenced to 120-hours community service and his driver's license was suspended for a year. He got it back two months ago."

"Gotcha. Is there anyone else in there with him?"

"Not that I can see, but I wouldn't bet money on it."

"Don't gamble, Tim. My life could depend on it. I'll call you when I get there."

I thanked him and hung up. Tim was barely seventeen, so I assumed he meant video games when he talked about *Splinter Cell*. I was never into gaming, but...

I shook my head and focused on the task at hand.

Tim texted me Mason's address, but I didn't move. I really needed a plan, and help, and not just "Big Iron." I glanced at the revolver on the passenger seat, the yellow streetlights reflected on its stainless-steel barrel, turning it to gold. I picked it up, checked it out. It was clean and oiled.

The cylinder was full minus one; it weighed a frickin' ton, but it was ready to go to work. But was I? Not hardly. I set the mighty weapon back on the seat beside me—there was no way it would fit into my holster.

I sat there, thinking, for a minute more. I had no PD to back me up. I was *it!*

Okay then, "It," stop screwing around and go get it done.

I heaved a sigh, supremely conscious of the pain from my injuries of that day, and I put the Sport Trac into dive and sped away toward the Mason home, already formulating my plan of attack.

Tim was right: the stealth entry idea made the most sense. I doubted the Mason guy had much experience holding hostages, but I also didn't know what the hell was going on inside his addled head, or how many friends he had with him. I was thinking two, maybe three. If so, I could probably handle them, but I couldn't risk it. More than three and Chelsea was as good as dead.

What could've made them do this? I wondered as I drove. *Henrietta Mason, the boy's mother? If so, why? And was it her son who murdered Sandra?*

I had a strong suspicion that the answer to that was yes.

But it makes no sense. And what about Voron? How, if at all, are they connected to him? Is he at the Mason home, with them, waiting for me? I don't think so. If he wanted to kill me, he would have done it back in Hangar Town, but he didn't. And if Voron's not involved, why take Chelsea?

I should've asked Jim, I thought.

There were too many questions, and too few answers. Well, there would be time for answers when Chelsea was safely back home.

I stepped on the gas. The best policy was always to go back to basics, take it one step at a time; focus on the most immediate problem, solve it and go from there, and that was to gain entry into the house without getting my ass shot off.

I decided to park the Sport Trac on the street a couple houses away from the Mason home and walk the rest of the way. The revolver did fit into my shoulder holster, but the barrel was too long and poked into my left side. Still, it was handier than tucking it into my pants.

Thankfully, the Mason's house wasn't located in one of those exclusive, fancy neighborhoods, so my somewhat shabby car probably wouldn't attract attention, I hoped.

I strolled along the street, my hands in my pockets, staying out of the light of the streetlamps as best I could, toward the house. I took out my iPhone and plugged in my buds, to keep my hands free and the screen dark, and called Tim.

"Are you in position, Harry?" he asked.

His voice sounded playful, but I knew Tim was taking it seriously. He hadn't been with me long, but he had a sharp mind, learned quickly, and always seemed to be in control of the situation. Better yet, it kind of tickled me, the idea of having a tech guy talking in my ear. It was so... *Mission Impossible*.

"Yes, I'm here," I replied as I stood near the stone-and-iron fence, some thirty feet away from the front gate.

The fence was partially hidden behind vines, but there were two bright lights on either side of the gate, so I figured my position was the safest point of entry. I looked around, checking for pedestrians. There was an elderly lady with a dog on a leash at an intersection some fifty feet away. I squinted in the half-light and determined she was walking away from me.

Good.

"What's the plan, Tim?" I asked.

"There are two cameras on your side of the house, both in motion; I have you on GPS, by the way. I can see you... well, not you, a green spot that... Hey, you moved. Now I can't see you. Where are you?" Tim said. I heard him tapping wildly on his keyboard, then he continued, "Okay, gotcha again. On my mark, you'll climb over the fence. I'll count to three. You'll have exactly eleven seconds. Can you do that, Harry?"

"How the hell old do you think I am?" I asked.

"No offense, Harry," he chuckled. "I believe in you. One..."

I zipped up my jacket.

"Two..."

I stretched my arms and legs.

"Three!"

I jumped up and grabbed onto the top rail, right between the spikes. The metal was cold, and vines scratched at my face, and despite the pain in my stomach, muscles, and arms, I pulled myself up, kicked with my feet, swung my right leg onto the top rail, and hopped over, landing on the soft grass.

"I see you," Tim said. "Find a place to hide, four seconds, three..."

I looked around. The house was about fifty feet away, and the first-floor windows were dark. I saw a camera under the roof, moving slowly from left to right.

Holy crap. I'm in deep...

"Damn it, Tim," I said as I dived to my left and lay flat on my face.

"What are you doing, Harry?"

"Burying my face in the frickin' grass. What d'you think I'm doing?"

I heard him chuckle, then he said, "There's a barbeque

pit about twenty feet away from you to your right. On my mark..."

I lay still, feeling the grass dampen my pants, feeling my sore shoulders like I never had before, and said, "Screw your freakin' mark," I whispered. "Aren't you watching the cameras, Tim?"

"I am. Don't worry. You're not on them, yet... Go!"

I ran to the grills and the low wall surrounding them, hopped over into the pit and stayed low. "Was this the plan?" I asked.

"Yes, actually."

"Lucky me," I grumbled. "How are we doing with the cameras?"

"You're now out of the sightline of one, but there's another one aimed at the patio, but you're well-hidden where you are, for now."

"Jeez, this Mason lady needs to fire her security company." *Maybe she should hire me.*

I crouched behind the low wall and made my way to the end of it. I said, "What's next?"

"You'll need to make a run for the house. Hold on. I'll tell you when."

"Okay."

I held, put my right hand on the top of the wall, getting ready to leap out. I peeked above the wall at the camera.

"I can see the top of your head, Harry," Tim whispered.

"Damn!" I ducked back down.

"One... two... three!"

I jumped out from behind the wall and ran for the house, almost on all fours like a frickin' chimpanzee, staying as low as possible. I made it and hugged the wall. I felt like Inspector Clouseau.

"You're doing good," Tim whispered. "Keep your head down and go around to the back door."

I did. Hugging the wall, I rounded the corner, keeping low as I passed one dark window after another. The back stoop was right there, just one window away... and then the lights inside came on. I froze.

"Are you at the door yet?" Tim asked.

"No," I whispered. "Someone turned the lights on."

"Outside, oh hey, what—"

"Shut the hell up for a second, Tim, and let me think... No, not outside; inside."

It was the kitchen window. I peeked. Someone was rummaging through the fridge, a guy in his late twenties or early thirties, huge, with long hair and glasses. He grabbed a six-pack of Coors Light and slammed the fridge door shut.

I said, "Tim, the Mason kid, does he wear glasses?"

Tim typed, then said, "Not according to his driver's license."

Okay! That's good. I thought, my mind racing. *Now we know there are at least two of them.*

The guy turned off the lights, went out into the hallway, left the kitchen door open, and walked up the stairs.

So, they must be keeping Chelsea on the second floor... or not. Geez, what the hell am I doing?

"I'm at the door," I whispered. "There are at least two of them inside, plus mother Mason, I guess. Surely she's not involved."

"Can you handle the door?" he asked, and then added, "What am I saying, of course you can. Anyway, I'm turning the alarm off... now."

I expected to hear a beep or a power-down sound, but nothing happened.

"Okay," Tim said. "The system is down."

"Are you sure about that? I didn't hear anything."

"Well, that's a good sign. The alarm is off, but you probably shouldn't make too much noise."

"Thanks, Sam Fisher," I said, smiling.

"Harry, you Googled Slinter Cell," he sounded delighted.

"I did. Now please, concentrate on what we're doing."

"Yes, boss."

"Don't... Oh hell, never mind."

I grabbed the doorknob with my right hand and aimed my left elbow at the small window next to the lock and gave it a none-too-gentle nudge. The glass shattered and I cringed: it sounded like a gunshot in the still night air.

I stood frozen, listening so hard my damned ears hurt, but I heard nothing except the blood rushing through my head.

Finally, satisfied no one had heard anything, I reached gingerly inside and gently unlocked the door.

"I'm in," I whispered and slid inside.

"Excellent. Find a place to hide, and I'll kill the cameras."

I sneaked across the kitchen, past the stairs that led to the second floor, and hid behind a tall cupboard in the hallway.

"The eagle has landed," I whispered, keeping it light.

"Huh?"

"Got myself a hiding place," I said, shaking my head. *Geez, do these kids today know anything at all?*

"Oh, good," he said. "Okay, killing the outside cameras... Now."

At first, for several minutes, nothing happened, but then I heard a commotion in the room above my head. Low voices, unintelligible words, but a heated argument, for sure.

Next came the banging of boots on the staircase. I tensed, listened; it was only one guy, but it was impossible to tell if it was the same Coors guy I'd seen in the kitchen.

He came down to the first floor and stopped. In my mind's eye I could see him standing there, looking around, listening for intruders. I stood rock still, pressed against the wall, out of sight on the far side of the cupboard.

"There's no one here!" he yelled.

I peeked around the cupboard. *Is the piece of crap gonna turn right into to the kitchen, or come left toward me?*

If he went into the kitchen, he'd find the broken window and raise the alarm, so I drew my Hogleg and readied myself for the inevitable: one way or another, I was going to have to neutralize the guy.

Fortunately, he came my way.

I flattened myself against the wall and waited. I was tempted to say "psst," the way they do in the movies before knocking the villain on the head, but it wasn't a movie, so I stayed quiet until the guy passed by the cupboard. He paid it no attention, and he didn't see me. I holstered the gun, stepped up behind him, hooked my right arm around his neck, grabbed the back of his head with my left hand and applied the classic choke hold.

The guy struggled hard. His instinct was to try to grab my right arm with both hands, instead of trying to kick or punch me. I didn't envy him. In less than twenty seconds he passed out, and his body went limp in my arms. I strapped his hands and feet with zip ties from my jacket pocket, opened the cupboard door, grabbed a wool scarf from a peg therein, rammed it into his mouth, and loaded him into the cupboard—which fortunately was used to store outdoor clothing, so there was space enough—and closed the doors.

"One down," I whispered. *But how many to go, I wonder?* "Going upstairs."

"Good luck," Tim said.

I reached the stairs. There were maybe a dozen steps and then a landing, and then another set of steps. Not ideal. I took the six-shooter from its holster and made my way slowly upward.

"Harry, hold on," Tim said.

I froze on the second step. "What?"

I heard him type, and then he said, "I'm trying to pull up the blueprints."

"What are you hacking now, the City Building Department?"

"Maybe. Do you want that floor plan or not?"

"Hit me," I whispered, worried that any minute someone would decide to check on their missing buddy.

Tim did his best to explain the geography of the second floor, and I basically understood what he was trying to tell me. I cocked the weapon, and the cylinder clicked around, placing a live round under the hammer, and that made me really nervous.

"All right, Tim," I whispered. "I'm going in."

31

I held the revolver raised to my face, its muzzle pointed at the ceiling, as I slowly, step by step, made my way forward along the second-floor hallway.

I heard muffled voices arguing, and then tiny whines, which I figured had to be Chelsea.

"I'm signing off, Tim," I said. "I need to concentrate," and I pressed a small button on my left earpiece, took them out and shoved them into my jacket pocket. I didn't want them getting in the way if it came to a hand-to-hand fight.

I stopped. There was a light shining under one of the doors.

"That you, Jerr?" a voice shouted. Then, quieter, "Where the hell is that guy?"

"Don't panic, man," another male voice said. "He's probably getting more beer, all right?" The tone was cocky. I figured it had to be Richard Mason.

"Screw the beer," the first voice said. "I got enough already. What we need is manpower, Ricky."

"What do you think we're doing here?" Ricky asked.

"I don't know, man! You started this shit! We're gonna

go to jail if we don't pull it off. What the hell is your plan, Rick? What do you want me to do? And now Jerr is gone you—"

"He's not gone, dumbass, he's downstairs. Go look for him if it makes you feel better, chickenshit."

They were arguing, which meant they were nervous, which also meant they probably didn't know what they were doing. That wasn't good. People who don't know what they're doing are hard to predict and likely to go off half-cocked. What was even worse, I didn't know what I was doing either: I'd have to be extremely careful.

"Don't call me chickenshit, Ricky. You got that?"

"Just go," Ricky replied. He sounded tired.

The door opened, and Coors guy stepped out. I quickly slid into what I hoped was an empty room. Fortunately, it was. It looked like a guest bedroom. I stood motionless in the shadows.

Coors guy must have heard me, because he stormed out of the room yelling, "Jerr! If this is some kind o' shitty prank, I swear..."

I heard him rush past my door. I set the revolver down on a dresser next to me—big mistake—opened the door and stepped out of the room—second mistake—planning to execute the same trick I'd pulled downstairs on the dude I now knew to be the erstwhile Jerr.

Coors guy was looking for his friend, and before I had a chance to grab him, he turned his ponytailed head in my direction.

"Hey," he barked.

And I immediately punched him hard in the nose.

I must've broken it, because his glasses broke into two pieces and fell from his face. He recovered quickly, covered his nose with his right hand, and began flailing wildly with his left.

"What the hell, Jerr!" he squealed, blood rushing through his fingers.

I grabbed onto his hand and pulled him into the room.

"What's going on out there?" Ricky shouted.

Coors guy mumbled something even I couldn't hear as I hauled him further into the room, until finally we both tripped over the corner of the bed and went down in a heap. His full weight crashed down on top of me like a landslide, pinning me to the soft carpet. His right hand was free then, and he turned over.

"Jerr?" he said. "What the hell are you doing?"

Coors had mistaken me for his unconscious friend. He rolled over, squinted at me in the darkness. I used the opportunity to drive an elbow into his cheek. He fell off me, and I scrambled to my feet, kicked him in the gut. The whole time my brain was sounding the alarm—it was an ugly situation.

I kicked the guy in the head for good measure and knocked him out cold. The struggle had taken maybe thirty seconds, but when I turned around, Ricky was standing in the open doorway, pointing a gun at me.

"Freeze!" he yelled, like it was some cheap cop drama.

In retrospect, it was laughable. In truth, it was pretty damn serious, so I did like he said. I froze. I began to raise my hands above my head, and it was then I realized the revolver wasn't in the shoulder holster.

Stupid, stupid, stupid.

Ricky turned on the lights.

"Who the freakin' hell are you?" he asked.

It took a few seconds for my eyes to adjust to the light.

Ricky Mason was tall, but not as buff as his friends. He

wore baggy jeans and a tie-dyed T-shirt that ended just above his knees and made it look like he was wearing a dress. His shoes were black-and-red Air Jordans. I bet he had a flat-billed hat somewhere, too.

"You a cop?" Ricky asked, pointing a small pistol at me.

"I'm not," I said.

"You that girl's boyfriend or something, old man?"

"Do I look that bad?" I said, more to myself than to Ricky. "I'm not her boyfriend, but I am here to take her home."

"Not happening, man."

"Oh, I think it is."

The guy seemed scared, but not so scared he wouldn't shoot me.

I said, "My people are watching the house, Richard."

"Ew. Only my mother calls me that. What do you mean they're watching the house, huh? We didn't see anyone."

"That's the idea," I said.

He took a small step back, his gun still on my chest.

"What's your name?"

"Harry Starke," I said calmly.

"You're that detective, right?"

"That's right," I said, and I glanced at the revolver on the dresser two feet away from Ricky, five feet away from me.

He saw it too, and said, "This your gun? Old school. Cool, huh?"

He grabbed it, hefted it, now pointed it at me and pretended like he'd fired it, making a weird noise with his mouth. Then he pointed both weapons at me. He was getting cocky, and also more dangerous. That frickin' six-gun was still cocked.

I said, "How about you lower those things, and we talk about it? Is your mother okay, Ricky?"

He frowned. "Whaddaya mean is she okay?"

"Did you hurt her?"

That line got a laugh out of the kid. "Why would I hurt her, dumbass?" But then he got serious. "Come with me, Harry Starke, and do it slowly. I ain't playing no games here, c'mon."

He took a step back into the hallway, and then another. I glanced back at his senseless friend and said, "You might want to check on your friend, Ricky. He's bleeding."

"That's his problem."

I couldn't argue with that, so I stepped out of the room after him. He backed up some more, then motioned for me to go down the hall. He steered me to the room where they were holding Chelsea.

I felt one of the guns poke the center of my back. I took the hint and opened the door slowly. Chelsea was tied to a chair in the middle of what I assumed was the master bedroom.

She looked up at me pleadingly, gagged with a piece of cloth. Her eyes were wet, dark mascara streaks on her cheeks. Behind her was a king-sized bed, and behind the bed was a huge fish tank full of colorful fish.

"Is the gag really necessary?" I said.

"Oh yeah, our girl Chelsea is a screamer," Ricky chuckled. There was something sinister about the laugh, not sadistic, but deranged, maybe. The guy was obviously under a lot of stress and that boded nothing good, of that I was sure.

"Are you hurt, Chelsea?" I asked.

The girl shook her head. I nodded.

"Take a chair, Detective Starke," Ricky ordered.

I walked over to the vanity table and grabbed a chair. It

was a bulky thing—white wood with a velvet cushion and velvet armrests.

"I'm not a detective, actually," I said. "I'm a private investigator."

Ricky widened his eyes in mock surprise. "How impressive! And look where it got you. Now, sit down next to the girl and tie yourself to the chair!"

"How do you propose I do that?" I asked, even though I'd already spotted the box of zip ties on the bed.

"Take the straps. Start with your legs. It's not that hard to figure out, *Detective*."

I set the chair three feet left of Chelsea, grabbed a handful of zips from the bed, sat down and looked up at Ricky.

"Why are you doing this, Richard?" I asked.

"None of your business, Detective, and don't call me that."

I reached down and used one of the straps to tie my left leg to the left leg of the chair; it was déjà vu all over again. The strap was a nylon strip with a ratchet closure. As I leaned down, I pushed my knee forward creating a gap between my ankle and the chair leg. It looked good from the front where Ricky was standing. If he didn't check... I repeated the process with my right leg and sat up, both legs pushed forward against the straps.

"Now, your hands."

I fixed my left arm to the armrest, arching my wrist slightly creating a similar though smaller gap between my arm and the rest, and I looked at him, expectantly.

"You want to give me a hand?" I asked, waving with my right hand.

"No tricks, old man, or I blow you the hell away!" Ricky said, and put my revolver down on the floor.

The other pistol was still pointed at my face, however, so I couldn't afford another mistake.

He stepped up to me slowly and took the last strap. I put my hand on the armrest, and Ricky looked at the strap, my arm, then the gun and quickly realized he either needed three hands or he had to put the gun down; he decided on the latter, and then some.

He smacked me upside the head with the pistol, taking me completely by surprise, then he dropped the gun and wrapped the strap around my arm. Before he could fix it, however, I headbutted him, jerked my right hand away, and grabbed his wrist. He tried to jerk it free. We struggled, and the chair tipped over sideways taking me with it. Ricky fell on top of me. He jerked his hand free and grabbed the gun, swung it toward me. I grabbed it and his hand and forced it upward. It fired.

I was stunned by the concussion. My left ear felt like someone had stuck a knife in it. The fish tank shattered and cold water poured down over the bed and all over me. I twisted the gun from his hand, ejected the magazine—mistake number three—and it fell to the floor.

"You son of a..." Ricky snarled as he pushed himself off and away from me.

I was wet, holding the gun awkwardly, my legs and left wrist still tied loosely to the chair. Ricky, now on his feet staggered backward, and said, "What's your problem, man? Chill out, will you?"

Oh yeah, he's frickin' crazy!

I pointed the gun at him, and then realized it was empty.

"Yeah, you're doing real good, Detective," he said, and he picked up the big revolver. "Does this thing even work? Should we find out?"

"Better not," I said. "It's over a hundred years old. It could explode in your face."

I dropped the empty pistol and put my free hand up.

Fish flapped around on the wet bed behind me. Chelsea moaned.

He stared at the old weapon for what seemed like an age, then he shook his head and said, "Forget it. I'm outta here, man."

He turned to Chelsea and said, "I'm gonna untie you now, sweetie. We're going for a ride, got it?"

She nodded.

"Where are you going?" I asked.

"Wouldn't you like to know, asshole," he said as he untied Chelsea with one hand, the muzzle of the revolver touching the back of her head.

"Careful with that, Ricky," I said. "You don't want to do something you're going to regret."

"Shut the hell up, dickhead."

He finished untying the girl, put a hand on her shoulder, and said, "Go slow, y'hear? Don't even think about running, or I'll blow your pretty little head off."

"You don't want to do this, Ricky. Think about it, man."

He pointed the revolver at me with a shaking hand, but that could just have been the weight of the pistol.

"I said shut up! I'm telling you, Detective, you keep runnin' your mouth and I'll frickin' kill you!" He looked again at the old gun, contemplating his chances, I supposed, then decided it wasn't worth the risk.

He shook his head and said, "It's too late for me anyway."

"What are you talking about?" I asked.

"You know what I'm talking about," he said with a smirk. "That's right, girl. I offed your momma!"

Holy crap, I thought, *the guy really is nuts.*

"It's not too late to make things right, Ricky."

"Yeah, it is," he said with a deranged smile, the big revolver shaking even more in his hand. "I'm out of here, Detective. Get moving, bitch."

He manhandled the crying Chelsea out the door and into the hallway. Me? He left me lying there, half tied to a chair, soaking wet and feeling stupid beyond words, and wondering how the hell I was going to stop Ricky and still keep Chelsea alive.

I listened as they descended the stairs. I rolled over onto my back, taking the chair with me.

My back erupted in a torrent of pain.

I grabbed the pistol and used the barrel as a lever to break the zip's ratchets on the tie that held my wrist. Then did likewise to those that held my legs, and that was even more painful than you can imagine.

I grabbed the magazine, slipped it into the pistol and slapped it home, racked the slide, and then I stood up... way too quickly. I almost shouted out loud as the pain speared through my twice-abused arms and legs.

I heard the two of them struggling toward the front door. Evidently, Chelsea wasn't going quietly. I prayed to God that Chelsea wouldn't put up too much of a fight. Ricky Mason was clearly unstable, not to mention reckless, and it was a miracle he hadn't hurt anyone tonight.

I sneaked across the second-floor hallway toward the stairs, my new gun clamped in both hands. At least I knew that gun worked—my damp back drenched in fish tank water served as a constant reminder of that. I wondered if the gunshot had been heard by the neighbors and then figured probably not; if they had, I'd already be hearing the sirens.

My phone buzzed in my pants pocket. I took it out, glanced at the screen: unknown number. I held still, listening to what was going on downstairs. I heard Ricky tell Chelsea to open the door; a moment later it slammed shut.

I answered the call.

"Starke."

"Hey, Harry, this is Bob Ryan," he said casually, and the sound of his voice helped me regain my focus.

"Perfect timing, Bob," I replied. "Remember how I said I might need backup? Well, I do. Now!"

"I'm listening."

I began to tell him what had happened, but even as I did, I heard Ricky's Wrangler roar to life. I had to cut it short.

"Listen, Bob," I said as I ran down the stairs. "Call Tim Clarke, my tech guy, he'll tell you everything. I'll text you his number."

I hung up without waiting for an answer, used Siri to write the text, sent it, and then slipped the phone back into my pocket.

As I crossed the hall to the front door, I kept my mind laser-focused on what I knew was coming next: a car chase. I sure as hell wasn't about to let Ricky get away with Chelsea.

I stormed out into the night in time to see the Jeep, trailing plumes of thick smoke, take off into the street.

"Ricky, stop!" I shouted, and I aimed my gun at the vehicle, my finger on the trigger, but I didn't shoot.

The guy was scared shitless, and opening fire on him would only freak him out more. The dark of the night didn't help, either. The Wrangler's impossibly bright LED head-lights made the body of the vehicle look like one big black spot with two red eyes... the rear lights.

My phone buzzed again. It was Tim. I put an earphone in.

"What's up?" I said, watching my target drive away out of the front gate.

"Mason is escaping!" Tim said.

"Well aware of that, kiddo. Can you track him? He has his phone with him, I think." It was a long shot, but... I took off running down the street to my car.

"I'll do my best. Call you' back as soon as I can. Go get 'im, Harry!"

I smiled, and he clicked off.

The Sport Trac fired immediately, purred like a sleeping tiger. I hit the gas, and the tiger roared, and the tires spun as I slewed the car in a controlled spin U-turn, and the beast took off after the Wrangler like a scalded cat.

Where the hell is he going? I wondered.

There were a couple of options I could think of. One: he was driving aimlessly, just trying to get away from the house, in which case the odds of me finding him without Tim's help were slim to none. Chattanooga is not a huge city, but it is big enough to get lost in.

But I remembered something that led me to believe that Option Two was the horse I needed to back: the black SUV I'd seen on my way out of Jim McDowell's property, and what Ricky'd said about more manpower. I was convinced that vehicle belonged to one or more of Ricky's friends: the two guys who'd put Robert Rainer in the hospital and attacked Jim: Buzz cut and his pal.

I had one of those weird feelings I seem to get in times of stress, that they'd never actually left the McDowell property and that was where Ricky was headed. He was going after reinforcements.

32

A s I sped through the darkness, I figured I had but one advantage: Ricky didn't know what I was driving. I'd parked on the street quite a piece down the road from the house, and, to the best of my knowledge, he hadn't, couldn't have seen the Sport Trac before.

I figured Ricky would be monitoring his rearview mirrors, and if he was... well, it was no time to worry about that. I drove fast, at times going way over the speed limit, playing checkers with other cars, and risking getting pulled over. In retrospect, it's amazing I survived that night chase at all.

My phone rang, and I took one hand off the wheel for a split second to press the button on my earphones.

"Starke."

"Harry, where are you?" Kate asked.

We had known each other a long time, and I could understand even the slightest inflections in her voice, like the agitation hidden behind a wall of badass-cop confidence.

"I'm in the car, driving. Why?"

"A little birdie told me you're on your way to getting yourself into trouble," she said, her voice soft.

Ryan... sonofabitch! I'll have words with that guy!

I said, "I'm already up to my neck in trouble, Kate. Has Jim McDowell called you?"

"No. Is he all right?"

"No! And I'm not surprised he hasn't called you. I told him to, but I don't think he can. Look, it's a very long story, Kate," I said, "and I promise I'll tell you everything..."

I made a sharp right turn, my tires squealing, and I spotted what I thought was Ricky's Wrangler in the distance. It was speeding away fast. Too fast, and I was surprised the police weren't already on his tail.

"I'll tell you everything later, Kate," I said. "I know who killed Sandra, and I'm on my way to Jim's house now. Not sure how much your little birdie told you, but I'll be needing backup sooner rather than later. But, Kate?"

"I'm listening."

"You have to be quiet about it. If I'm right, I'm going into a hostage situation," I said, hoping for her understanding.

"Harry, if you're right, I can't keep it quiet. I can't even take the risk that you're not right, you know that."

"Yeah, I do, and you're right, but, please, no sirens, no media, no helicopters. The suspect's name is Richard Mason, and he has Chelsea McDowell. I'm in pursuit."

She took a moment to process the information. "Holy cow, Harry. You should've told me sooner!"

I should've, but I hadn't, but now wasn't the time to argue about that.

I said, "Yeah, should've, and I'm sorry, but Jim was supposed to call you and... Look, I have it under control," I said as I ran a red light.

Oh yeah, sure you do!

"I'll call you when I get there, okay?"

"Okay. We're on our way."

She hung up. *This is good*, I decided. I had no obligation to report to Kate or the CPD—and it was still my investigation—and I figured it was better for me to stay one step ahead and remain in control of the situation. One thing I wasn't sure of was if Kate could handle Henry Finkle. If he was with her—she'd been having problems with him ever since I left the department—he might be trouble.

It's already after eleven o'clock and he's off-duty by five-thirty, so maybe I'll get lucky.

Ricky was passing cars like he was a NASCAR driver, even swerving into oncoming traffic, his horn blasting as loud as his headlights were bright. I had to stay with him, so I too stepped on the gas, breaking every kind of speed limit and not even trying to blend in anymore.

Careful, Ricky, I found myself thinking. The last thing I wanted to see was his ugly Wrangler crash into innocent bystanders and hurt who knows how many people.

I pressed on, hard, shrinking the distance between us down to less than a hundred yards. I figured he had to know I was there. I considered trying the Pit maneuver, but dismissed the idea almost immediately. My Sport Trac was doing a sterling job, but it wasn't equipped to ram an off-road Jeep Wrangler.

The closer we got to the McDowell home, the more the traffic increased. I turned on my hazard lights, mashed the horn and put my headlights on high beams and flashed them—it was the best I could do without a police siren, but it proved to be effective: the traffic seemed to part like the waters before Moses.

Despite what logic dictated, I hoped that Ricky would arrive at Jim McDowell's house safely, before the CPD could drive him off the road. Chelsea was in the Wrangler, and I'd bet all of August's millions that Ricky hadn't bothered to strap her in.

What a frickin' mess... One thing I was grateful for: at least Ricky was focused on driving and not on shooting. If he ever decided to use that damned great cannon...

I continued to follow him, my crappy make-shift light show blazing, and then the first police cruiser showed up in my rearview mirror. Its red-and-blue lights illuminated the street behind me, and he was catching up with me, fast.

I took my hand off the horn and grabbed my phone. I called—who else—Sergeant Kate Gazzara.

"How is it looking, Harry?" she asked, and I knew right away the situation had been reported to her.

"So far, so bad," I replied. "Unfortunately, Kate, this ain't a social call. You've got to call your guys off my tail. Or at least tell them to hang back. I don't want the crazy fool to wreck and hurt—or kill—Chelsea."

"I'll try. I've sent two unmarked cruisers to Jim's address. All seems to be quiet there."

"How close did they get?" I asked, my heart pounding.

"Parked at the curb out on the street."

"Good. Keep them there and tell them to get out of sight. We don't want to spook the crazy son of a bitch. I'm following him. We'll be there in five."

"I'm on my way too," she said. "Harry, I hope you know what you're doing."

"You know I do, hon," I replied. "Call you back."

I hung up. Did I know what I was doing? Well, mostly. I did have a plan in mind, sort of, which, if the CPD didn't intervene and a certain someone showed up on time, would wrap this case up with a nice purple ribbon and a thank-you card. Yes, there were still too many moving parts but having everything—and everyone—in one place, the right place, would help a lot.

Ricky made a hard right, cutting the corner onto the street that would eventually take him to Jim's house, and I drifted after him, almost spinning out of control. And then I dropped back, let him go. I knew where he was going, so I didn't need to chase him anymore. Thank goodness!

Kate's people in the unmarked cars must've been good at their job, because as we neared the house, there was no sign of them, nor did I spot any blue-and-white cruisers anywhere on the approaches to the mansion. Neither had Ricky, because he drove in a straight line and then carefully turned into the open gates of Jim's property. I didn't follow him, but instead double-parked on the street and stepped out.

I still had Ricky's pistol in my holster, with a very limited amount of ammo, or so I thought. I ejected the mag and checked: *twelve, less the one he'd fired, eleven left, wow!* I looked, for the first time, at the weapon. It was a Taurus 9mm, cheap, but reliable. I hoped I wouldn't need it, but now I felt a little better.

In the movies, the action hero is expected to go in guns blazing, dealing lead left and right. In real life, nobody wants to shoot anyone. Nobody wants to kill another human being. And most of all nobody wants to get killed, me most of all, and I didn't have a vest, didn't even own one. *I bet I do tomorrow if I make it through the night... Good title for a song, that.*

It was at times like that, I realized how small and silly our issues were. Three people were already dead and how many more left injured? And all for what? Money? I scoffed out loud as I stood on the empty and mostly dark street outside the McDowell mansion, pondering these questions, waiting.

The wait was not long. A black-and-yellow Dodge Caravan slowly rolled down the street and stopped next to my car, and the driver hit the emergency lights. A few seconds later, Bob Ryan stepped out, paid the driver, and the taxi left.

I shook his hand. "Thanks for coming, Bob. I wasn't sure you'd show up."

"I've saved your ass twice now, Starke. Gimme some credit here," he said and chuckled, and I smiled with him.

"Fair enough, Bob, fair enough. How'd it go at the station? Finkle give you a hard time?"

"That guy's a piece of work. I can see why you quit the PD. Now Sergeant Gazzara, on the other hand—"

"Hey," I interrupted, giving him a pointed look that said, *that's my woman you're talking about, so watch it.*

Ryan got the hint, grinned, nodded and said, "Gotcha! So, what's the plan, chief?"

"We go in and get Jim and Chelsea out of there, neutralize the bad guys, and save the day," I joked, as my mind churned. "Then, I go home and pour myself a tall glass of Laphroaig, and cook steaks for me and Kate."

"As fine as all that sounds, Harry, you'd better give me some usable intel on the situation. How many are there? What's the house like?"

I knew what he meant, and I was calculating. I said, "Do you have a gun?"

"Don't need it," he replied, eyeing the house from afar. The view wasn't great. "Do you have access to their cameras?" he asked. "That guy Tim talked my ears off about how he's hacked every surveillance system in the city."

"Of course. Hold on a minute."

I took out my phone, put buds in my ears, and dialed Tim. As I waited for him to answer, I saw a couple of cruisers cut off the road at the end of the street. Same deal at the other end. Thankfully, they were far enough away, and kept their sirens mute and emergency lights off—just a couple of black silhouettes blocking the streets. I looked up at the night sky and listened. No helicopters either. For now, at least.

"Harry?" Tim said in my ear.

"Yeah. I'm at McDowell's house. What happened to you? You never called me back. Where are we on the McDowell security cameras?"

"He must have dumped his phone, is why I didn't call you back. As to the cameras..." he said, yawning.

I glanced at the screen of my phone and realized it was twenty to midnight. No wonder.

"Whew. Excuse me," Tim continued. "The security system at the house is offline, all of it, cameras, alarms."

"Phone lines?" I asked.

"Silent," he said.

"Okay, that's either good, or very bad," I said.

"Whichever it is," Ryan said, even though he couldn't hear Tim's side of the conversation, "we better move fast."

That, I couldn't argue with.

"All right, Tim, thanks. There's nothing else you can do for us now. Go get some sleep, okay? Your mom must be going crazy."

"Yes, Harry, and thanks," he said.

I hung up.

"We're blind, Bob," I said, taking the buds out of my ears and shoving them back in my pocket. "Two hostages, and, I think, three or four bad guys, likely armed. The Mason guy has a six-shooter."

"A six-shooter, are you kidding me?" he asked, his eyes never leaving Jim's house in the distance.

We stood in the street watching the house like a couple of stalkers.

"Jim McDowell's gun. Colt 45, 1895 Frontier model."

"Classic. Reliable. Eminently lethal, in my experience. Handheld elephant gun," Ryan said.

There was something inhuman about the way he talked about it, void of emotion. I'd been around ex-military guys, cops, even hitmen recently, but that night Bob Ryan gave me chills.

"So, what do you say?" I asked.

"I say we quit hanging around like a couple of nerds at a prom and go on in." And, without further ado, Ryan started toward the open gates of the property.

I followed.

"Hey, slow down, Ryan," I said, and he did. "If we're doing this together, it's my op. You're the backup, remember?"

He frowned. I could tell he had ideas of his own. Tough!

I walked ahead, Ricky's pistol in my hand. We didn't walk up the driveway but instead took a side path that took us around the house, behind a four-car garage, and on to an immaculately landscaped, tastefully lit Japanese Zen garden, with a small koi pond, a fountain, and a rock garden.

"Fancy," Ryan remarked.

I didn't answer. I scanned the area instead. The seemingly endless backyard was devoid of human life. We stepped onto the patio. I motioned for Ryan to keep down. This area was well-lit. I raised the Taurus, anticipating an attack. But all remained quiet.

I turned to look at Ryan. His hands hung loosely at his

sides. He winked at me, seemingly unconcerned. There, in the half-light from the house, he kind of reminded me of the Hulk's younger brother—if he had one—and I didn't envy anyone who got in his way. He too scanned the back patio and the pool area.

"All clear," he said.

"Evidently," I said.

"Are we going in, or do you wanna take a swim first?" he asked sarcastically.

"Maybe afterward," I retorted and put a hand on the sliding glass door. It wasn't locked. I slid it silently aside and stepped inside. Ryan followed close behind.

We split up, cleared the first floor, tiptoeing methodically from room to room, closing doors softly behind us, until we reconvened at the bottom of the main staircase, next to the door to the room where Jim had given me his revolver. I opened the door, hoping to find another one.

No such luck. It was a small room, barely a closet.

"Nothing?" Ryan said in a low voice.

"No."

"Upstairs?"

"Oh yeah."

"Is there another way up?" he asked.

"There should be another staircase down the hallway to the right, for the help."

"Damn, it gets fancier by the minute. Okay, Starke, I'll take that route, since I'm your 'backup.'" He made quotes with his fingers.

"Sounds like a plan," I said, and I stepped toward the main staircase. "You sure you don't need the gun?"

He raised his clenched fists and smiled a sinister smile. "Got everything I need right here."

He disappeared down the hallway, and I started up the

stairs, for the second time that day holding my pistol pointed at the ceiling, stepping softly and constantly watching my back.

I heard voices in the distance, upstairs, muffled by the thick walls. Men's voices, several of them. At the top of the stairs, I stretched out my arms, the gun now pointing forward, my eyes locked on the sights.

Ryan appeared at the end of the hallway. He nodded. I nodded back and stepped forward. He did the same. We met halfway, stopped, and listened together.

Jim's house had two wings: the one which Ryan had come through was smaller and dedicated to guest bedrooms; the other was where the McDowell's master bedroom and other family bedrooms were located, which made it the perfect place to keep hostages—single point of entrance, a convenient overview of the outside from the windows and balcony.

I motioned for Ryan to follow, and we silently approached the door to the first room. I listened intently but couldn't tell if there was someone behind that door or beyond it. I looked around and was about to move on to the next door when Ryan opened the door.

33

"What are you—" I whispered.

The door creaked, and then he crouched and popped his head inside.

He glanced at me. "All clear."

I scowled at him but raised my gun and followed him into the room. What the hell else was I supposed to do?

We found ourselves in what had to be some sort of family room. The couch could've easily seated a party of ten, and the plasma TV on the wall was at least a hundred inches. There was also a large dining table and a frickin' pool table. I never would have taken Jim McDowell for a guy with a man-cave, but it wouldn't have been the weirdest discovery of the investigation.

The muffled voices now came from the other side of the door on the opposite side of the room, and both Ryan and I crouched behind either end of the couch, flanking the door.

"What's the plan, chief?" Ryan whispered.

"Working on it. You better find something to fight with."

He rolled his eyes and grinned at me. "I have all I need, Starke," he said, "but just maybe..."

"Oh, come on, get on with it," I said.

He nodded, and crouching, he half-ran to the pool cue stand on the wall and picked out the longest, thickest cue there was, as well as half a dozen pool balls, which he put in the pockets of his jacket.

I watched him, taking mental notes. Not about the methods, but about the man and his habits. Using a pool cue and balls seemed barbaric, but it also told me that Bob Ryan wasn't afraid to get down and dirty when it came to trouble... and I liked that.

I could use a man like that.

I stood, stepped quietly to the door, and listened. Ricky was inside, talking in erratic, mumbling sentences, as he explained what had gone down at his mother's house. He mentioned my name, as well as Chelsea's and Jim's. Another, older voice, confirmed his version of the earlier events: they had come in, beaten the crap out of Jim and snatched Chelsea.

You bastards...

But who were they talking to? I had a pretty good idea, at this point. Ricky Mason had no business running around killing people. He was thirty-three, born into money, still living with his mother—he was obviously a momma's boy—driving a cool car, going out with hot girls, drinking expensive booze... But he wasn't capable of managing the events that had transpired over the last several days. And by "managing" I mean pulling the strings, giving orders. Only one person I could think of was capable of that, and that person was in there now, listening to her son explain to her how things had gone sideways so quickly.

I tiptoed over to Ryan, who had the pool cue at the ready, like a spear.

"Got that plan figured out yet, Starke?" he said.

I could tell he was impatient. I could relate; I was too.

"It's simple. There's our door," I waved with my gun. "We got the element of surprise, but I suggest one of us goes out onto the balcony and takes a closer look." I nodded in the direction of the French window.

"Gotcha," he said, and he started toward the door.

"I see," I said. "Okay, I'll give you the signal when to go in, got it?" I said, starting toward the balcony.

Ryan nodded.

I opened the balcony door as quietly as possible and stepped outside.

The night was dark, the sky a field of countless stars: still no police helicopters, nor could I see any blue lights in the distance. I breathed steadily, deeply. We were almost there.

Hostage situations could stretch on for hours, but I had a feeling this one would be resolved quickly, if not elegantly. Ryan struck me as a guy who would shoot—or swing a pool cue—first and ask questions later, if at all, and I myself wasn't too fond of Ricky and his windbreaker-wearing buddies.

I took a few cautious steps toward the next room, hugging the wall and holding my pistol up by my cheek. The light pushed through the windows, and shadows danced on the balcony floor. I heard Ricky's voice.

"It's not my fault, Mom, all right? I wasn't there!"

There was no reply, and Ricky grunted and paced the room.

From the echo of his voice and steps, I estimated the room to be maybe a third of the size of the one I'd just left. A private lounge or a bedroom, maybe Jim and Sandra's special room, who knew? I inched closer to the window.

"Richard, calm down, *now!*" Henrietta Mason said. Her

voice was nowhere near as pleasant as it was when I first met her at Belle Edmondson, but it was just as fake. "Sit down and shut your mouth, young man," she hissed, her voice high-pitched, sounded "nasty" is the only word for it. She was showing her true nature.

I peeked in. Jim was sitting side by side with his daughter on a huge bed, their wrists tied together with a pink and glossy *Victoria's Secret* tassel belt. Their mouths were taped shut. For a moment, they both sat so still that my heart skipped a beat; they looked as if they were dead, but then Jim turned his head and looked at their captors. They were simply too tired to struggle.

Ricky did as he was told; he sat down, crashing into a large armchair in the corner, half-turned away from me. His lip was split, his left cheek red.

Geez, not only did his mother likely make him kill Sandra, she physically abuses him, too. What kind of woman beats the crap out of her thirty-two-year-old son?

I moved another inch to the left, and I saw them: two large, hefty guys dressed in black shirts and jeans, their hair cut short, one of them sporting a fanny-pack. They looked grim, aggressive. I'd seen similar faces in too many mugshots —if it came down to a shootout, they'd be the first to pull the trigger, and that meant I would have to be quicker.

Henrietta Mason stood between them, arms crossed on her chest, staring at her son, who appeared to be weeping in his chair. She wore sweatpants and a shapeless shirt, and her hair was brushed back and fixed in a tight bun on top of her head.

"You're an embarrassment, Richard," she said. "This is all your fault. You were supposed to scare them, not... Are you crying? Pull yourself together, you idiot! How the hell old do you think you are?"

"Leave me alone," Ricky pleaded.

Hell, I almost felt sorry for the guy.

The window was floor-to-ceiling, but part of it was blocked by a cabinet, so I crouched and made my way to the sliding patio door. My plan was to fire a shot—hoping the police on the street wouldn't hear it and come charging in like Custer and the 7th Cavalry. All I wanted was to divert their attention and give Ryan the nod to enter the room to jump the kidnappers.

I aimed the gun in the air and glanced over the cabinet. My finger tightened on the trigger... and then all hell broke loose.

The door flew open, woodchips flying in all directions, and Ryan stormed in. What happened next took maybe five... six seconds at the most, in real time. I watched it in some kind of mental slow motion that seemed to enhance each of Ryan's fluid and calculated movements.

He rushed into the room, smacked one of the two windbreaker goons on the ear with the cue, reversed it and stabbed him in the stomach with the tip. The goon folded, retching his guts up and, before he even hit the floor, Ryan was dealing out damage to the other goon.

He hit him twice with the thick end of the cue: the first blow hit him dead square on the bridge of his nose. I couldn't hear it through the glass, but the strike must have broken it. The second blow landed smack in the center of his forehead. It was as if Ryan pushed the off button; the goon fell backward, crashing to the floor, almost at the same moment as his friend.

All of this happened before Henrietta even had time to turn around, but Ryan wasn't bothering with her, not just yet. Ricky was already half out of his armchair when Ryan turned to deal with him, and there it was: Ryan fulfilled my vision. He threw the pool cue like a spear, thick end first, and it hit Ricky dead center of his chest—THUMP! It was a hammer blow. Ricky flew backward into the chair, the wind knocked out of his lungs, and he began hyperventilating.

Henrietta turned away, her eyes wide, her teeth bared, and she ran to a sideboard on the other side of the room where, as we found out later, the big Colt .45 was stashed in one of the drawers.

Ryan went after her, and he was a lot quicker than she was. He seized her right wrist, jerked it, spinning her around, her free arm flailing wildly. He tripped her. She fell to her knees. He yanked her arm up her back, forcing her down onto her stomach. He grabbed her free hand and wrenched it around behind her back, and then he held both her wrists in place with just one hand.

"You there, Starke?" he called.

I stepped inside through the balcony doors, my gun still raised. Looking back at that night, it had worked out for the best, but at the moment, I was pissed... No, I was furious.

"What the hell was that?" I snapped.

"Hostage negotiations?" He smirked.

"You could've gotten them killed!"

Ryan kicked one of the goons. "These assholes? Big loss. I didn't, though, did I?"

Henrietta looked up at me, her eyes wide. "Harry! Save me from this monster! He broke into the house and... and..." She stopped when she realized I wasn't buying it.

Ryan listened, then he said, "Lady, you're something else, that's for sure."

"Just give us a minute to secure these clowns," I said to the two wide-eyed captives on the bed, "and we'll be with you, okay?"

They both nodded.

I scanned the room, and then I put my gun away. Ricky was choking in the chair. He was in trouble, so I stepped over to him and put my hands on his shoulders.

"Slow, deep breaths, Ricky. That's it... a couple more... good. You're going to be fine."

I grabbed the landline phone from a nearby nightstand, jerked the cord from the wall socket, then from the base, and used it to secure Ricky's hands behind his back. He protested, struggled, still coughing violently, but ultimately he relaxed in the armchair, breathing hard but subdued.

"Got some more?" Ryan asked.

Henrietta still fumed on the floor, but I could see in her eyes that she knew it was over.

I grabbed a couple of Jim's shirts from the closet and tore them into strips. I tied the Provost first, then the two goons, and then we turned our attention to the two captives and released them.

Jim and Chelsea almost fell off the bed, grabbed each other, both crying uncontrollably, gabbling how much they loved each other.

I looked at Ryan, nodded toward the door, and we stepped out to give them some privacy.

Less than a minute later, the door opened and Chelsea ran out, threw herself at me, wrapped her arms around my neck, and through tears said over and over, "Thank you, thank you, thank you."

"It's okay, Chelsea. It's over. You'll be fine now, and your dad, but you should thank Mr. Ryan, here. He took them all down."

She let go of me and grabbed him, thanking him profusely. He looked at me over her head, obviously embarrassed. I grinned at him. Then it was my turn again. Judge

McDowell had joined us too, and he grabbed and hugged me. Embarrassed, me? Not hardly.

Finally, I managed to disentangle myself from Jim's embrace and stepped away.

Jim said, "Thank you, both of you, but especially to you, Harry. I knew I could count on you."

"Just doing my job, Jim. I'm just glad you're safe, and I'm sorry you had to go through it all."

And I was, but I still had questions that needed answers. If I was going to get them, now was the time, before Kate and her crew hauled them all away.

"There's something I need to do," I said. "Could you guys wait out here?"

"I'll keep an eye on them, Harry," Ryan said.

I stepped back inside the bedroom, closing the door behind me. Then I crossed the room to where Henrietta was seated on the floor, her hands tied behind her back.

After I sat down on the edge of the bed, I locked my hands together in front of me and looked down at her.

She glared up at me, "What?"

"Was it worth it, Henrietta?" I asked.

She didn't answer, just continued to stare at me through hate-filled eyes.

I said, "Sandra McDowell is dead. Robert Rainer is in the hospital in a coma. Your son is going to prison for the rest of his life, and so are you."

She glared at me. "No, he isn't."

"Yeah, he is, Henrietta," I said. "The murder of Sandra McDowell, kidnapping, assault with a deadly weapon, the list goes on."

She glanced past me, at the balcony, and then at her son. Then she sighed, shook her head, looked down at the carpet, then up at me, her eyes watering, and said, "He didn't kill Sandra. Those two knuckleheads did."

"Is that so?"

"It is if I say it is," she snapped.

"That's not how the courts work, Henrietta," I said.

"This is never going to court, Harry. I know people who wouldn't even look twice at a plebeian like you! They'll vouch for me and my boy. I have an alibi. I—"

I raised a hand to silence her. "Enough. Why did you do it? I don't care who actually killed Sandra, because you were behind it. Why did you do it?"

She remained quiet for a long moment, no doubt trying to figure out what story to tell me.

"Henrietta," I said, "it's over. If you confess, they might go easy on Ricky. Not these two." I glanced at the two unconscious, bleeding goons. "If Ricky didn't kill her, he might go free," I lied.

She looked at me. "Can you guarantee a deal?"

"I'm not with the police, so I can't guarantee anything. It's out of my control, but I can put in a good word for you."

"I only asked them to talk to her," she said, finally. "I told them to scare her, these two stupid clowns." She cocked her head at the goons.

"Why?" I said.

"The night she died—"

"Was killed," I corrected her.

"The night Sandra was killed we, the school board, worked on the budgets for next year. During a meeting break, we got to talking, me and Sandra, just the two of us. Her daughter will graduate next year, and she said she wanted her to get into a good university. But she was concerned about Chelsea's chances. I offered her... a smooth transition, a guarantee, you could call it."

"Meaning?"

"I'd grease a few palms and acceptance at a top school was guaranteed... for a fee of two hundred and fifty thousand," she said.

"A fee?" I said. "You mean a bribe?"

"We're talking Ivy League, Harry. Guaranteed. Some people would kill for it, but not Sandra. She was outraged, said she was going to expose me."

"And some people would kill to keep it a secret," I added.

She shrugged. "I did what I had to do," she said, and then she broke. "I'm not proud of it. I have an idiot son to look after." She glanced at Ricky and then continued, "It wasn't supposed to go this way. I tried to convince her to keep quiet, but no, our law-abiding Sandy McDowell wanted to discuss it with her husband first. Judge McDowell! And I know what she meant when she said "discuss," too. She would've ratted me out. They would've sent me to prison!

"So I sent Ricky and his friends after her. They were just supposed to talk to her, scare her, but the idiots killed her. And then what was I supposed to do? Look at him, for God's sake." She looked up at me, tears rolling down her face, her eyes pleading.

"Why Chelsea? Why did you have Ricky kidnap her?"

She looked up at me, her eyes mere slits, and said, "To put pressure on the old man, of course. Sandra was on the phone the minute she left the board meeting. I figured she was talking to her husband, the judge, telling him everything... I needed to make sure he kept his mouth shut, especially after they killed her." She heaved a deep breath, then continued, "Nothing, nothing went right. They killed Sandra and everything went to hell."

"Did you get that?" I said.

Henrietta blinked. "Huh?"

"Every word of it," Kate said in my ear.

Yeah, I didn't mention it earlier, but before entering the room, I speed-dialed her and whispered, "Listen." And she did.

"I recorded it, Harry. What's the situation?"

34

"We have it under control, Kate," I replied. "Jim and Chelsea need medical attention, and so do the bad guys."

"Oh, please, don't tell me... Okay, we're on our way. Wait, who's 'we'?"

I stood up and took a few steps away from Henrietta to where Ricky was still panting in the armchair.

"Oh, didn't I mention it?" I said with a smile. "Bob Ryan's here too. Since he's my intern, figured I'd show him the ropes, you know?"

"I can't even begin listing everything that's wrong with that sentence, Harry. Okay. Stay put. We'll be there in a minute."

"Ok, but keep the recorder running."

I glanced outside then and saw blue-and-red flashes in the distance, and then sirens blared. The cavalry was on the way. I needed to work quickly. We had Henrietta, but I still needed more answers.

"How are you doing, Ricky?" I asked.

He looked pained, both physically and emotionally. I couldn't blame him.

"I didn't do it, honest," he mumbled.

"Speak up, Ricky."

"I didn't do it. I didn't kill Sandra."

I watched his eyes, trying to see the lie and failing. "Then, who did? Was it your mom?"

He shook his head. "Jerr did."

"Jerr?" I asked, even as I remembered the guy I'd knocked out back at the Mason house.

"Jerry Colston. He hit her on the head."

"And you drew the 'V' on the road?" I asked.

"Yeah. I saw it online, about that killer who's being executed. But Jerry killed her. Did you kill him, back at Mom's place?"

"No, I didn't," I said, turning away so he wouldn't hear what I said next.

"Kate?" I whispered. "There are two guys at Mason's address, they're—"

"We got them, Harry," she said calmly.

"You did?"

"Tim called me as soon as you left there, and I sent a cruiser over to check it out. They're in custody."

Five minutes later, Henrietta Mason and her son were also in custody, along with the two goons she'd hired to beat up Robert Rainer. Later, she would claim he was blackmailing her, but gave it up when she realized it wasn't working.

She knew that Rainer knew about her scheme and tried to silence him too. He did recover from his beating, and he did testify against her in the College Admissions Scam hearing six months later. That case was the first of many, and by itself resulted in dozens of arrests.

Henrietta drew multiple sentences totaling eighty years in prison for her many crimes. Jerry Colston was sentenced to life in prison for the murder of Sandra McDowell. Ricky was tried as an accessory, got five to ten years, and another ten years—the sentences to run consecutively—for kidnapping Chelsea and her dad.

The two goons each got five years for the assault on Rainer and their involvement in the kidnappings, but both were released after a couple of years for good behavior. I never saw them again.

But I digress. I wasn't yet finished with Jim McDowell.

I waited and watched with Jim and Chelsea—they were seated in the back of an ambulance—as the goons and the Masons were loaded into police cruisers and taken away, and then I turned to Jim.

"Thank you again, Harry..." he began,

I held up my hand and shook my head.

"Don't mention it... Listen, I need to talk to you in private, if you have a minute."

"If it's about the money, I—"

"We'll figure that out later. It's about Mary Turner."

Chelsea gave him a look. "You should go, Dad. Tell Harry the truth."

I smiled at her.

I put a hand to Jim's elbow and helped him to stand and step out of the ambulance.

"So," I said. "Tesak is in custody and the rest of Voron's pals are dead, but he is still out there, Jim."

"I know, Harry. I wouldn't worry about it."

"Mary's his daughter," I said. It wasn't a question.

"She is," he admitted.

"Explain."

Jim took a breath. "She was only five when I put her

father, Voronov, away. She was at that hearing, of course, and it broke my heart. I thought it was another of Voron's tricks, at first, that he was trying to apply emotional pressure. But those two loved each other. Still do."

"So, you adopted her?" I asked.

"Never formally, no. But I did take care of her. Vlad had done some horrible stuff, but I saw no reason why the child had to suffer for the rest of her life... I think prison has reformed him. I wouldn't invite him to my next birthday party, but I'll always care for Mary."

"That's very kind of you, Jim."

"Speaking of birthdays... Voronov told me you'd crack the case, and he said you'd come asking about him sooner, rather than later."

"He said that?" I smiled.

"He's good at reading people. He called it the first time you two met."

"Impressive. Did he say anything else?"

"He told me you'd figure it out, but he also asked me not to make your life harder."

"Nice of him," I said, unable to hold back the sarcasm.

"It's his granddaughter's birthday this weekend. Voron is with her, at our country house, and so is Mary."

"I appreciate it, Jim. I'll make sure they're taken care of. Mary and her daughter, I mean. Can't speak for Voron."

"I understand. He does, too."

We stood quietly for a minute, each of us contemplating the other and... perhaps our own lives too.

"Have a good night, Harry," he said and rejoined Chelsea in the ambulance.

"Take care, Jim," I said. "I'll see you later."

Someone tapped me on the shoulder. I turned. It was

Kate. She wrapped her arms around my neck and hugged me.

"I was so scared," she whispered into my ear, so that no one else would hear.

"Me too, sweetheart, me too. But it's over now. Well, almost."

She pulled back. "What do you mean?"

"I'll tell you in the morning," I said, and I gave her a small kiss.

We wrapped things up at the McDowell mansion and then headed to the PD for the inevitable and interminable interviews and statements.

Kate and Finkle—oh yeah, he was there too—listened first to my story, then Ryan's, then the recordings Kate had made at the McDowell mansion via my iPhone, and so it continued until finally we'd all had enough and it was decided to continue the next day. I said nothing about Voron's whereabouts. I figured he had no more than a few days left to live... *Hell, let him enjoy them, and his family. What can it hurt?*

It was almost three in the morning when I left the PD. Tomorrow would be a good day, I hoped.

I wished Ryan a good night and sent him on his way in an Uber... *Geez,* I thought, shaking my head as I watched the car pull out onto Amnicola and turn right. *Where the hell did he come from?*

35

"You want a ride, big boy?" Kate asked as I watched the Uber's taillights disappear.

My Sport Trac had been impounded, as had Ricky's gun, so I had little choice. I grinned at her and slid into the passenger seat.

We picked up a couple of orders of biscuits and gravy at an all-night restaurant, went home to my place, ate the food, showered together then fell into bed, too tired to do anything but hold each other and whisper sweet things to one another. I don't even remember the moment when I drifted off.

I woke up maybe four hours later, but I felt fresh and focused. I made breakfast, and when Kate joined me in the kitchen, I said, "Remember how I said it's almost over?"

She grabbed a cup of coffee. "Yeah. Is there more you want to tell me?"

"Where do I start?" I said.

And then I shared what Tim had found about Mary Turner, and then repeated everything Jim had told me, and at eleven o'clock that morning, we climbed into Kate's cruiser and sped away, picked Bob Ryan up on our way, and took the highway, escorted by two blue-and-white cruisers.

Jim McDowell's summer house was located on Chickamauga Lake, about forty minutes away from the city. We settled in for the drive, and Ryan fell asleep right away.

An ex-military guy had once told me that one thing he'd learned in the army was "sleep when you can, eat when you can." Advice to live by, really.

Kate and I talked a little, but we were both still in cop mode, and there was little emotional capacity for a casual chat, especially with the red-and-blue lights going crazy on the dash.

I explained in more detail and from a more personal point of view how our "operation" had gone—another trial run before our official statements later—including Ryan's heroics with the pool cue. I wanted to make sure his role in it would be appreciated.

"Harry," Kate said, almost to herself, "you shouldn't risk your life like that."

I think it was a plea rather than a comment. Boy, if either of us knew what the future held...

"I can't make any promises." I smiled as I said it, but then spoke seriously. "This is my job now, Kate. What am I supposed to do? Call the cops every time there's a problem? You know I can't do that. Look, I think I've put together a good team, and I know they have my back. You, Ronnie, hard-ass Ryan back there... With you guys I can do anything; the sky's the limit."

"Wow, Harry, that's actually pretty inspiring! Is it too late for you to switch to speechwriting?"

"You can joke, but I'm serious."

"I know..."

We drove in silence after that, and I had no idea what

she was thinking about. Me? I was thinking about Voron, and a tiny part—the paranoid part—of my brain was telling me we could be walking into a trap. There was no reason why Jim would have sent us into one, but I had an image in my head and I couldn't get rid of it: we arrived at the summer cottage only to be ambushed by more Russian hitmen. I chased the thought away.

"How much longer?" I asked.

"T-minus ten minutes," Kate joked, but nobody laughed.

I felt for the unfamiliar gun in my shoulder holster—my backup Glock 17 from the safe at home—and, once again, I hoped it would remain there.

It was just after noon when Kate left the highway and turned onto a dirt road that took us to a row of lakeside summer cottages, spaced a couple hundred feet apart. All had boat docks, most with expensive cruisers moored to them.

Jim's was a moderately-sized one-story house with a wide porch and an old John Deere tractor parked at the side of the driveway. We parked at the front of the house, and the six uniformed police officers dispersed around the property, guns drawn.

It was a nice spring morning, and although the lake breeze was chilly, the sun was warm, and clouds were few. I walked up to the house and knocked on the front door.

"Voron!" I yelled. "I know you're in there!"

No response. I drew my gun and went around the house.

Music was playing, some cheerful melody I didn't know, like a kids' show theme, or maybe just a song they taught kids at school, I wasn't sure. But as soon as I saw Mary's daughter, I put my pistol away and turned back.

"Kate! There are children here!" I said.

She responded immediately. "Lower your weapons!" she ordered.

The officers did, and the three of us—Kate, Ryan, and me—proceeded to circle the house and crash the kid's birthday party.

The air was filled with a wonderful smoky smell. Mary Turner was playing with Penny. Voron was at the grill, flipping burgers and hot dogs. He waved when he saw us.

Kate said, "Vlad Voronov, put your hands up!"

The three of them stared at the three of us and, for a moment, no one moved or spoke.

Then the Raven said, smiling benignly, "Please, you are welcome!"

"I said, hands up!"

Voron did as he was told, but the smile never left his face.

I said, "Good seeing you again, Voron."

"Likewise, Mr. Starke. And this must be Sergeant Kate Gazzara? Nice meeting you too, my dear." He looked at Ryan. "And we, you and me, we have already met, haven't we?"

Ryan wasn't amused. "Yeah, we have. Can't say I enjoyed the experience."

"I do apologize," the one-time assassin said. "That was a... an unfortunate misunderstanding... no?"

"I'd say so," I offered.

"You are under arrest, Voron," Kate said, skipping the pleasantries.

"Of course, of course," Voron agreed. "May I just ask you not to cuff me in front of my family?"

We glanced back at Mary, who embraced her daughter. Both were scared and confused. They thought they'd have more time together and, even today, I sometimes wonder if I should've given them at least another day to catch up, to live like a normal family. I could have. I didn't need to tell Kate where he was when I did... but I didn't know.

Kate motioned with her head, and Voron followed us behind the house, out of his girls' sight. She cuffed him.

"Thank you," he said earnestly.

"So, you weren't lying," I said.

"I wasn't, Mr. Starke. I know I don't deserve it. Freedom, family... I discarded all that a long time ago. But they haven't, and they do deserve it, Mr. Starke."

Kate didn't say anything, nor did Ryan—they were skeptical—but Voron was looking into my eyes, and I believed him. I almost felt sorry for all the mess that had gone down: the Sorbonne, Hangar Town, Voron's dead friends. Had Sandra not been killed, Voron would've escaped just as his friends had planned, and spent a few days —his last days— with his family. Oh, well.

"Good luck, Voron," I said as Kate led him away.

Because of his escape and the proceedings that followed, he was executed two months later instead of five days. Mary visited him once more on death row. She and her daughter moved into Jim McDowell's house soon after Voron died. I think it helped them all to come to terms with Sandra's death, as well as to work through their experiences. Mary really did become Chelsea's older sister in time.

"What will happen to us?" Mary asked, when Ryan and I approached that Saturday noon in December 2008.

"Nothing," I said. "Jim and Chelsea are safe, and I know they both want you to be there for them."

She breathed a sigh of relief. "Thank God!"

Ryan said, "If it makes you sleep better." And he walked away.

What the hell did that mean?

Kate returned after the cruiser took Voron away and gave Mary and Penny a ride to the McDowell mansion. Ryan and I took a cab to my office, where the team was already assembled, the smell of coffee filling the air.

When we entered the conference room, Ronnie, Jacque, and Tim stood up and applauded us, huge smiles on their faces. Ronnie even whooped a couple of times.

"That's enough of that, geez," I said as I shook hands.

"He does it again," Ronnie said.

"Yeah, but I couldn't have done it without you guys... and without this guy right here."

Everyone looked at Ryan, who smiled thinly.

I said, "Team, meet Bob Ryan. Bob Ryan, team."

They shook hands and introduced themselves, while I watched. The chemistry seemed to be there: they were already joking about Tim's obsession with computers, and I even heard Ryan refer to me as "the boss." Which reminded me...

"Bob, can I speak to you in my office?"

He shrugged but followed me. When he closed the door behind us, I said, "Look, Bob, I know I've called you my intern. It was our cover story, but I've been thinking. Would you like to—"

"Yeah," he said, "I would."

"I wanted to say, would you like to work for me? I could use a man of your talents in the agency."

"Yeah. Yeah, Harry, I'd be down with that. When do I start?"

"You're serious?" I asked, thinking maybe he was joking.

"Dead serious, Harry. I'd like to work for you."

"Don't they need you back in Chicago?"

He shrugged, pretended to be thinking, but then he

said, "Nope. It's just me, and since I'm an ex-cop, emphasis on the ex, I'm in the market for a job."

"It's settled then! Let me catch up with Ronnie next week, and we can figure out your back pay. You did save my ass, after all," I said.

"Some might say twice." He grinned.

"Some might say that, yeah." I said, sarcastically.

I smiled, shook his hand, and we returned to the conference room and rejoined the rest of the team.

I cleared my throat and said, "Team, please welcome our newest member, Bob Ryan."

They exchanged glances, and then it was round two of applause, handshaking, and introductions. I was right. It was going to be a good day, and then a good week and then... Well, you know the rest, or at least most of it. There are some adventures I might tell you about, but for this one, all you need to know is that day my team and my company became one man stronger.

36

T hree *Weeks Later*
       Bob Ryan sipped from a tall glass of beer. The
cafe Starke had chosen wasn't that fancy—which,
as Bob had noticed, was a pattern with Starke—and that was
just fine. Bob was hidden under an umbrella, out of the
weak winter sun, and the cold beer made it all the more
enjoyable.

He took another sip.

He wasn't nervous, no. The opposite—the last few
weeks have been the calmest he'd ever felt. He'd secured a
job, bought a car, and was house hunting. Life was good.

His new boss wasn't bad, either. Harry had a couple of
tough cases on his plate, and he was more than willing to
share the workload. The pay was nothing to sneeze at,
either.

Speak of the devil, he thought as a Maxima rolled to a
stop at the curb, and Kate Gazzara and Harry stepped out.
Harry wore khakis and a black shirt, while Kate had opted
for jeans and a white top. They looked like the perfect
couple.

"Hey, guys," Ryan said. "Beer?"

"I'll take one," Harry said.

"I'm driving," Kate said.

She hugged him, and the three of them sat down. Ryan ordered two more beers, Harry some food, and Kate a latte.

"So, what's the occasion?" Ryan asked. They hadn't told him prior to the meeting, but he could tell from their attitude that they had good news.

Harry produced a white envelope and put it on the table until his beer arrived.

"This is for you," Harry said, passing Ryan the envelope. "Picked it up this morning at the post office."

"What is it?"

"Oh, for Pete's sake, open it," Harry said impatiently.

Ryan took the envelope, tore it open along the short side.

"Well, we've been working together for a while now..."

"Not even a month."

"Almost a month," Harry corrected. "So, I thought it was time to make it official."

Ryan took out the papers, one of which had a plastic card glued to it. It read: *Tennessee Licensed Private Investigator*. Below was Bob Ryan's name, and the name of Harry's detective agency.

"Welcome aboard, Ryan," Harry said.

Harry saluted with his beer glass, while Kate saluted with her coffee. Ryan did the same, with a huge grin on his face.

"Wow, this is legit, Harry. I guess I'm a real PI now, huh? Look out Sam Spade."

"The realest of PIs, Bob," Kate said, and she chuckled.

"What about you?" Ryan asked her. "You ever think of

going independent? You could help me keep Harry in line." He winked.

Kate shook her head. "This will sound weird, but I love being on the force. I don't think I could just up and leave. I serve the people, you know? And me work with Harry? Get outa here!"

"I hear that, sister," Ryan said. "That's a good attitude to have, for sure."

"Yeah," Harry said, "especially when you consider that her boss is Henry frickin' Finkle."

They drank some more, and they talked some more about nothing in particular, until Kate got called into the office—third homicide that week, a possible serial killer situation—and she left, congratulating Ryan once again. She hopped behind the wheel of Harry's Maxima and disappeared into the sunny winter morning.

"You're a lucky man, Harry."

"I think so," Harry agreed.

"Any plans for making *that* official?"

"Any particular reason you're asking, Bob?" Harry asked, with a smile.

"Just making conversation, Harry. I wanted to thank you, by the way, for taking me on as your... Do I even have a title?" he asked with a smile.

"No need to thank me, Bob, you earned it. And your title..." He thought for a minute, then said, "How about Chief Investigator?"

Ryan grinned. "Works for me!"

Harry raised his third glass of beer.

Ryan seconded it with his own salute, and they drank to it.

"Good times," he said.

"Well, yeah, and many more to come, I hope," Harry

said. "Look, I need to go home for a while. Kate's picking me up later," Harry said. "See you at the office tomorrow?"

"Absolutely. I'll be there."

Harry left seventy bucks under his glass, but Ryan said, "Hey, boss, my treat today, since I'm officially employed and all."

"Won't say no to that, Bob. Enjoy your afternoon."

They shook hands, and Harry caught a cab, leaving Bob alone at the table.

Ryan watched him go, an enigmatic smile on his lips.

His phone had been on the table the whole time, but now he reached into his pocket and produced a flip-phone, flicked it open and thumbed a number he hadn't used before, nor would ever use again. It rang for a long minute, and then the person on the other end picked up.

"Speak."

"It's Ryan. I'm in."

Instead of hanging up, Ryan broke the phone in half and put it in one of the dirty glasses. He left some cash on the table, finished his beer, and walked away.

FINALLY

"Genesis, a sure to be bestseller and 5-star action mystery-thriller and find out for yourself - what are you waiting for?" *Rosemary- Amazon Reviewer*

Would you like a free copy of the first book in my new best-selling Harry Starke series, Genesis? Just sign up for my newsletter and I'll send you a copy. Copy and paste this link: BookHip.com/VLCVQQ

Thank you:

I hope you enjoyed reading this story as much as I enjoyed writing it. If you did, I really would appreciate it if you would take just a minute to write a brief review on Amazon (just a sentence will do).

CPSIA information can be obtained
at www.ICGtesting.com
Printed in the USA
LVHW082248180819
628092LV00015B/1219/P